W9-BJC-960

“My time is all yours, until my truck is fixed,” Connor said.

“Better be careful,” she said. “I’ll have you so busy that you’ll forget about leaving.” She grinned, then handed him the cabin key.

“Thank you,” he said quietly.

The gratitude in his eyes took her aback, so Keeley gave him a breezy smile to lighten the moment. “No problem at all.”

“No—I really mean it.”

He rested a hand on her shoulder as he spoke, and she stilled, unable to take another step as a gentle warmth seemed to travel straight to her heart.

“It seems like a lifetime ago when I was around anyone as thoughtful and caring as you are, and I don’t think anyone around here even realizes how special you are.”

Flustered, she didn’t know what to say. He was so tall and utterly handsome, though it was the man inside who drew her.

“Thank you. For everything you’ve done for me.” Their gazes locked. “I’ve spent a lot of years being angry that my prayers went unanswered. But now I realize they have been all along… They’ve brought me to you.”

A *USA TODAY* bestselling and award-winning author of over thirty-five novels, **Roxanne Rustand** lives in the country with her husband and a menagerie of pets, including three horses, rescue dogs and cats. She has a master's in nutrition and is a clinical dietitian. *RT Book Reviews* nominated her for a Career Achievement Award, two of her books won their annual Reviewers' Choice Award and two others were nominees.

Books by Roxanne Rustand

Love Inspired

Aspen Creek Crossroads

Winter Reunion
Second Chance Dad
The Single Dad's Redemption

Rocky Mountain Heirs

The Loner's Thanksgiving Wish

Love Inspired Suspense

Big Sky Secrets

Fatal Burn
End Game
Murder at Granite Falls
Duty to Protect

Visit the Author Profile page at Harlequin.com for more titles.

The Single Dad's Redemption

Roxanne Rustand

If you purchased this book without a cover you should be aware that this book is stolen property. It was reported as "unsold and destroyed" to the publisher, and neither the author nor the publisher has received any payment for this "stripped book."

Recycling programs for this product may not exist in your area.

ISBN-13: 978-0-373-71965-5

The Single Dad's Redemption

Copyright © 2016 by Roxanne Rustand

All rights reserved. Except for use in any review, the reproduction or utilization of this work in whole or in part in any form by any electronic, mechanical or other means, now known or hereinafter invented, including xerography, photocopying and recording, or in any information storage or retrieval system, is forbidden without the written permission of the editorial office, Love Inspired Books, 195 Broadway, New York, NY 10007 U.S.A.

This is a work of fiction. Names, characters, places and incidents are either the product of the author's imagination or are used fictitiously, and any resemblance to actual persons, living or dead, business establishments, events or locales is entirely coincidental.

This edition published by arrangement with Love Inspired Books.

® and TM are trademarks of Love Inspired Books, used under license. Trademarks indicated with ® are registered in the United States Patent and Trademark Office, the Canadian Intellectual Property Office and in other countries.

www.Harlequin.com

Printed in U.S.A.

Many are the plans in a person's heart,
but it is the Lord's purpose that prevails.
—*Proverbs* 19:20–21

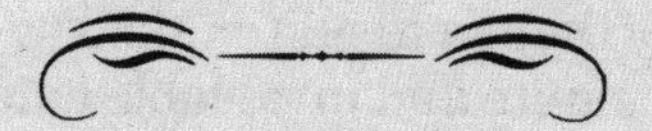

With many thanks to author Lyn Cote,
my "sister of the heart," who has been
such a wonderful friend from the day
I began my writing journey many years ago.

And many thanks to editor Melissa Endlich,
for her astute and invaluable guidance.
I appreciate you more than words can say!

Chapter One

Looking up at the roiling black clouds, Connor Rafferty turned up the collar of his denim jacket and lengthened his stride.

Aspen Creek was definitely a tourist town. The far southern edge held a scattering of truck stops, bars and shabby houses, but the original part of town was more upscale with six blocks of stately old Victorian homes and brick mansions. At least ten of them had been converted to elegant B and Bs with small, discreet signs on the sidewalk offering off-season rates.

Rates that would be far beyond his very limited means.

He strode on, over an arched stone bridge spanning a wide creek and through the six-block-long downtown area, feeling as if he'd stepped back in time.

The town was all about historical flavor. High on their fancy elevated facades, the quaint stone-and-brick, two-story buildings all proclaimed dates in the mid-1800s; the street signs were lettered in antique script.

What had probably once been a main street filled with empty storefronts and other evidence of a dying town was now brimming with stores geared toward the yuppie tourist trade. Gift shops, pretty little tea shops, restaurants, fancy women's clothing boutiques and a bookstore. For the outdoor sports enthusiasts, a variety of stores offered gear from fishing, kayaking and canoeing to skiing, backpacking and biking.

A single, massive bank on Main, with a plaque embossed with the year 1864 on the cornerstone facing the sidewalk, looked as if it could withstand World War III.

Somewhere on the north edge of town he'd find a cheap strip motel and, a mile farther, a campground with modern facilities, according to the tow-truck driver who had dropped Connor's pickup at Red's Mechanic Shop & Wrecker Service south of town.

Connor hadn't intended to make this stop in eastern Wisconsin on his way from Montana to Detroit, but major engine problems had certainly changed his plans in a hurry.

This was exactly the kind of thing he didn't need, with just a few hundred bucks in his pocket, nearly seven hundred miles to go and a burning need to reach the son he hadn't seen in five long years.

Five *irreplaceable* years in the life of a young boy. And five years of worry about how well his ex-wife was taking care of him…or not. A familiar surge of anger burned through his chest at the thought of what he and Josh had both lost, and the God who had ignored his prayers.

Josh had been only four when Connor went to prison. Would the child even recognize him now?

A blinding bolt of lightning struck the steeple of a white-clapboard church a few blocks down and a deafening *crack!* shook the sidewalk beneath his feet. The tentative patter of rain turned to a deluge in earnest, pouring off the brim of his Resistol Western hat and soaking through his denim jacket.

Just as quickly the rain turned to an onslaught of marble-size hail.

He ducked into the first entryway on his right and stepped into a dimly lit store. Soft classical music drifted through the cinnamon-and-coffee-scented air.

It took a moment for his vision to adjust to the warm golden and amber lighting of flickering candles, plus a dozen or more stained-glass lamps and chandeliers displayed around the store. An avalanche of what his grandma had always called "pretties" seemed to fill every millimeter of space. China. Glass doodads. Frothy lace.

Fancy stuff at odds with the steady plink of water hitting a galvanized bucket sitting on the floor by the end of the front counter.

He couldn't have felt more out of place if he'd suddenly found himself on Mars.

A slender young woman behind the cash register stared at him in shock.

He belatedly jerked off his hat and ran a hand over the two-day stubble on his face. "Sorry, ma'am. I…I just stepped in to get out of the hail," he murmured. He reached behind himself for the door handle, acutely aware of the puddle forming beneath his battered Western boots. "Sorry 'bout the mess."

"No—don't go." She slipped around the corner of the front counter, deftly avoiding the bucket on the floor. Her shoulder-length, shiny blond hair swung forward against her cheek as she motioned to the white wrought-iron table and matching chairs displayed by the front window. "Just listen to that storm out there. Have a seat. Coffee? Hot tea? I've even got fresh shortbread cookies."

"Really, ma'am, I—"

"Sit." She smiled, her green eyes sparkling. "At least for a while. If you go back out and get yourself struck by lightning, I'll forever feel it was my fault."

He awkwardly took the chair closest to the door and

glanced around for a place to hang his hat, then settled it on his knees.

"Coffee?"

He nodded. "Uh…thanks."

She bustled to the coffeemaker at the end of the front counter and soon returned with two steaming mugs of coffee and a tray of cookies, each with a little purple-frosting flower on top.

"You can be my taste tester. This is the first time I've made lavender shortbread, and the coffee is a new brand of Irish cream."

The aroma of the coffee was pure bliss. The first bite of cookie was like an explosion of rich butter and a delicate flowery flavor on his tongue. Nothing in his memory had ever tasted as good.

She grinned at his reaction as she took the chair opposite his and offered her hand across the table. "Keeley North."

"Connor. Connor Rafferty." He hadn't seen—much less talked to—such a pretty woman in more than five years, and the brief contact of her delicate hand in his sent his mind reeling back to a different time and place. Back to when he'd been a carefree man who worked hard and found pleasure in simple things.

Privileges he'd never appreciated until he was behind bars. Privileges and opportunities he would never fully regain.

In his former life, he might have asked this charming woman to meet him for coffee…or maybe even dinner, in the hope of getting to know her better.

Now he knew there was no point.

Once he revealed his past, a woman like this one would run the other way.

Shaking off his dark thoughts, he looked up and found

she was watching him with an expression of concern. Had she asked him something?

"Are you all right?" she asked, her voice gentle and warm.

Today's stress and exhaustion after fourteen hours behind the wheel of his pickup, plus several more on the side of the road with engine trouble, had turned his bones to lead.

"Just…a long day."

"You aren't from around here," she said as she leaned back in her chair and studied him over the rim of her coffee cup.

"Nope." Clearly, she already knew that from the way she was looking at him. Maybe she'd already figured out he wasn't just some average guy, either. He shifted uneasily, feeling as if his prison number was stenciled on his denim jacket.

Outside, hail battered at the windows in heavy sheets and continuous lightning lit up the sky like the Fourth of July. He took a swallow of coffee, savoring the heat as it slid down his throat.

"Texas, right?" She cocked her head. "Or maybe Oklahoma? I love the accent."

That was what she'd noticed? He jerked his gaze up to meet hers. "Texas, ma'am. Though it's been a long while."

"Just passing through?"

"On my way to Detroit."

"But then you fell in love with our pretty little town and decided to stay," she said with a twinkle in her eye.

He shifted uncomfortably. "Not exactly. My truck broke down five miles from here."

Her eyes widened a little at that. "Sorry. At least you got into town before this weather hit, right?"

"Yeah." Though the weather was the least of his problems.

"Were you towed to Red's garage—south side of town?"

"Yep."

"He does good work, but he usually has quite a backlog. When will he get it done?"

"A couple weeks…maybe three."

"Ouch. Sounds about right for Red's, but that can't be very convenient." She drummed her fingers on the glass surface of the table. "So I suppose you'll be renting a car to continue on?"

If only he could. This trip to Detroit meant everything to him. He had to find his ex-wife, Marsha, and son before she made good on her threat and disappeared again.

But he'd planned on smooth sailing, not a massive mechanic's bill coupled with extra weeks of motel and food expenses.

After buying a fourteen-year-old Dodge Ram diesel in Montana, the cash in his wallet had already run low and running up debts with no employment in sight would be risky. Renting a vehicle to reach Detroit and then returning for his truck later wasn't even a dim possibility.

"No. I…guess I'll have to wait for the repairs." He dredged up a wry smile, knowing the customers who patronized a fancy store like this one could probably replace a vehicle like his without a second thought.

Not that they'd ever own such an old beater in the first place.

He rose, reached for the thin wallet in the back pocket of his jeans. "What do I owe you?"

"Nothing. Everyone who walks in is welcome to the coffee." She studied him, her gaze boring into his until he felt as if she could see clear into his deepest thoughts. "I don't mean to pry…but will you just be doing the usual tourist things around here while you wait, or might you be looking for some work?"

Who would even hire him, given his past?

"I..." Heat crawled up the back of his neck as he faltered then swallowed his pride. "I could use something temporarily, since I have to stay in town awhile. But I don't expect I'd find anything like that around here."

Biting her lower lip, she hesitated. "Maybe. Our busiest days of the year are next weekend, and I'm short of help. If you're interested, I might have a temporary job for you here. Even a week or two could help us both."

Startled, he glanced around at the antiques, the china, the delicate bits and pieces displayed in every nook and cranny. He managed a short laugh. "You're kidding, right?"

"I'm afraid you won't find much of anything else in a town this small. Our population is less than four thousand and there's no manufacturing here. Without the agriculture throughout the county and our tourism, the town would die."

"What about construction?"

"There aren't any big companies based here—I think the closest are maybe thirty miles away or so."

"That's it?"

"We've got a few small, independent contractors in town—father-and-son teams who only do remodeling, though every time I try to schedule a reno project they're all booked for months ahead." She sighed. "I don't know if they're looking for extra help, but I sure wish they would so they could work faster."

He nodded, the weight of his situation growing heavier by the minute.

"Jobs around here are mostly at the resorts, restaurants and shops," she continued. "But we're on the verge of tourist season, and the high-school kids have probably nabbed every seasonal job they can find."

He felt his heart sink to the pit of his stomach. He'd

once earned six figures a year on the rodeo circuit, but he'd liquidated all of his assets for legal fees while fighting to keep his freedom and he'd still ended up in prison.

Now it sounded as though he'd be lucky to find even a minimum-wage job slinging hamburgers or sweeping floors. "So there's not much hope, then."

"You never know." She went behind the counter and pulled a newspaper from a shelf underneath. "You're welcome to take this. The classifieds are on the back pages."

She rummaged through a file drawer along the wall behind the counter, withdrew a sheet of paper and handed it to him with the newspaper. "Here's an application, just in case you decide to apply here."

Words failed him as he glanced at the fancy doodads in the store. Just looking at it all made him feel big and awkward and claustrophobic, and made him want to step outside to take a deep breath. "I don't think this would be a good fit, ma'am. But I appreciate the offer."

She shrugged. "Keep me in mind, just in case. The job wouldn't be that hard. I stock gifts, antiques and work by local artisans, with some gourmet foods and such thrown in. Running the register is easy."

He felt his jaw drop at her willingness to take a chance on someone she'd just met, and a warm ember of something long forgotten flickered to life in his chest. He hadn't remembered that people in the outside world could offer trust so easily. Then again, she didn't know where he'd been for the past five years.

"You could be making a big mistake, offering a job to a complete stranger."

"I won't be, if you fill out the application," she said with a tentative smile. "Believe me, I *always* follow up on references and do background checks. Anyway, I've been saying some prayers, so maybe this was meant to happen. You could use some short-term work and, at the very least, that's what I need. How much better could it be?"

If she only knew.

He hesitated then shook his head. "I appreciate your offer. But I think I'd better look around town a little more, if it's all the same to you."

Long after Connor disappeared down the sidewalk, Keeley stood at the front bay window of the store and stared after him. What had just happened? There were a number of big-name horse breeders and trainers in the county, but an honest-to-goodness Texas cowboy had never, ever, walked into her store—boots and all.

Much less one who looked like *that.*

Tall and muscular with broad shoulders and raven-black hair, he'd made her heart stumble the moment he'd walked into her store. His dark five o'clock shadow had drawn her attention to his strong jaw and the flash of white, even teeth when he'd briefly smiled.

He looked like someone who could take on any challenge with the laconic, easy grace of a man straight out of the Old West. But it was his long, dark lashes and those silver-blue eyes that had made her heartbeat stumble. The emotions lurking in those stunning eyes spoke of pain, and loss, and suffering, and had called to her at the deepest level.

She was still standing at the window, frozen in place, when her friend Beth Stone, owner of the bookstore down the street, waved at her from the sidewalk and came inside.

"You look a bit shell-shocked. Is everything all right?" Propping her umbrella in the entryway, Beth tucked a stray strand of chestnut hair behind her ear and scanned the shop. "But of course not. This is Edna's last day. Is she already gone?"

Keeley blinked, still reeling from the cowboy's unexpected appearance. "She came in earlier to say goodbye and is well on her way to Florida. The store already feels empty without her."

"She was always such a hoot. And she was so cute—always imagining herself a matchmaker but never quite getting it right. She was certain her nephew Ken was just the man for you."

Keeley stifled an inward cringe. For all her wonderful qualities, this had been the one small catch when working with Edna.

She and her elderly cronies in this small town enjoyed arranging introductions and pushing their prey along the road to wedded bliss. But Ken was bald, paunchy and old enough to be Keeley's father, with four wild teenagers and—the biggest barrier of all—he wasn't a believer.

Edna had tried to work her matchmaking skills on Keeley and Ken for the past two years, but it was *so* not going to happen.

"She always had a good heart, trying to make people happy," Keeley said tactfully.

Beth chuckled. "So true. I'll miss that, and I'll miss teasing her about her beloved Wisconsin Badgers. So... any prospects for her replacement?"

"I did have a drop-in of sorts, just before you arrived." Keeley felt the back of her neck warm. "A cowboy stopped in—"

"A cowboy? Here?"

"From Texas, apparently. He's heading for Detroit but had car trouble and will be around for a while."

Beth's gaze drifted to the lace displays. The glass case showcasing antique jewelry. The pretty dried-flower arrangements. "This is the most girlie shop in town. You really found a guy who'd be good at this sort of thing?"

"Not exactly." Keeley managed a wry smile. "You and I both know how bad I am at hiring people. The only time I ever got it right was when I found Edna."

She'd wanted to hire a replacement early so she and Edna could both work on training the new clerk before the annual Aspen Creek Antique Walk next weekend—the busiest sales days of the year and the crucial beginning of spring tourist season.

But her first hire had failed to show up. The second had found making correct change an impossible feat and saw customers as a bother when they interrupted her personal phone calls. The third had lasted two days and then walked out for good—apparently with a number of lovely antique rings and bracelets in her pocket.

And since then not one person had answered her advertisement in the paper. Not *one.*

Keeley shuddered, remembering all the reasons why she desperately needed help, and soon. Long-term. Temporary. *Anyone.* The first honest, dependable person she could find.

That brought her thoughts right back to the tall, dark and unwilling cowboy.

"So this guy stopped in. And?" Beth prompted.

"I'd just finished praying. I've been so frustrated trying to find a new employee that I just turned it over to God and promised to hire the very first person who walked in—if they wanted a job."

Beth's eyes sparkled. "And?"

"The cowboy came in to escape the rain, and it was such perfect timing that I thought maybe it was a sign from above. But he wasn't interested."

Beth's face fell. "Too bad."

"Exactly. I need to be here to run the store, but you know what it's like with my dad these days. I might have to leave at a moment's notice, if he needs me. Know any-one who wants a job?"

"Believe me, I would send them right over. It took me three whole months to replace my last assistant manager." Shaking her head in commiseration, Beth set a small white bakery box on the counter by the cash register. "I brought this for Edna's farewell, but she's already gone. So if it's any consolation, here's something from Sweetie's Bake Shop. Nothing like a nice sugar overload to lift your spir-its, right?"

"At this point, I sure hope so. Can we share it?"

A heavy roll of thunder vibrated the oak flooring be-neath their feet and Beth frowned. "I'd better get back to my store before the deluge starts again. Have you heard the severe-weather warnings on the radio?"

"Rain and more rain. A chance of flooding for the next five days. Just what we need."

Beth laughed at that as she headed for the front door and picked up her umbrella. "I'll be praying for you, Keeley. Hopefully your next applicant will be *perfect*."

Chapter Two

Keeley North hadn't been kidding.

By five o'clock Connor knew that looking for a job in Aspen Creek and actually finding one were two different things. He'd walked every block, checking store windows for Help Wanted signs. If seasonal jobs had been available this spring, they'd already been snapped up.

The lodging situation wasn't any better.

He hadn't bothered checking out the B and Bs in the grand old homes, but even the handful of seedy strip motels in town were too expensive. At least the campground would be cheap. Set along the banks of Aspen Creek a mile north of town, according to the tow-truck driver, it was just five bucks a night and even included a building with showers.

He could pitch his one-man backpacking tent and manage on basic fare cooked over his camp stove for the next two weeks, no problem there. He'd already done the same and enjoyed the open sky for two nights on the road while on his way to Detroit. Even a primitive campsite was better than prison walls.

Now he sat hunkered over the classifieds and a cup of coffee in a truck-stop café at the south end of town, looking for any opportunities he might have missed. He'd passed some beautiful horse-breeding farms and training facilities on his way here—rolling hills, white fences, fancy barns. One, the Bar-B Quarter Horse Ranch about fifty miles back, had made him long to saddle a green colt once again. Those were the kinds of places where his background would be a perfect fit.

But none of them was advertising for help.

The only jobs listed were those he wasn't suited for. Nurses. Home health aides. Day-care providers. A nanny for infant triplets.

The last one made him shudder.

He glanced heavenward, a rusty prayer forming in his thoughts. Then he just sighed, dropped a couple of bucks on the table and stood.

The kind and loving God of his childhood Sunday-school days sure hadn't bothered to answer his prayers whenever he'd really needed help, and Connor hadn't been on speaking terms with God for a long, long time. Why would He care now?

Connor shouldered his duffel bag and headed north on Main toward the campground, thankful that the rain had stopped.

He pulled to an abrupt halt.

Across the street, an old black New Yorker sedan pulled away from the curb and lurched to a stop in the middle of the street. Then the elderly driver laboriously backed up over the curb and swung across the sidewalk, apparently planning to execute a slow-motion three-point turn using the empty lot next to Keeley's store.

But the car kept going back.

And back.

Until it bumped into a tall wooden ladder propped against the flat roof of the two-story building.

Then the car lurched forward into the street and lumbered away, the driver clearly oblivious to the destruction in his wake as the ladder teetered…then crashed to the ground.

Connor shook his head in disbelief. Did that old duffer even have a driver's license? At least no one had been *on* the ladder, which now lay in splinters.

Movement at the top of the building caught his eye and he lifted his gaze to see Keeley standing on the flat-topped roof with a dumbfounded expression, a hammer in one hand and her other hand propped on her slim hip.

His heart took an extra beat.

"Dad," she shouted, clearly exasperated. "Come back here!"

The car continued down the street at a turtle's pace.

"Dad!"

The sidewalks were deserted; no other cars were coming down Main. Keeley's attention swiveled to Connor. "Hey," she called down to him. "Can you help me?"

Connor walked across the street to the empty lot and studied the splintered ladder. "I think this one is toast. Got another one somewhere?"

She mumbled something he didn't make out and he couldn't help but grin up at her. He couldn't see what she'd been working on, but she was the cutest handyman he'd ever seen, bar none.

"I'll take that as a no. Want me to call 9-1-1? The fire department or the police?"

"Oh, no. *Please* no," she said fervently. "I'd never hear the end of it. Neither would my dad, and he would not handle it well, believe me."

"Was that ladder the only way up there? Isn't there an inside stairwell?"

"There is, but only to the second floor. And right now,

the trick is getting from here to there. The old iron fire-escape ladder is too weak to use."

"Isn't that a fire-code violation?"

"Of course it is. Just last week I had a contractor look at leaks in the roof and give me an estimate on replacing the fire escape."

The lowering sun backlit her cloud of honey-blond hair, making it gleam with sparkling highlights, though her face was cast in shadow. He suspected she was frowning at him, maybe debating her next move. "So how can I help?"

"Could you go into the store and up the stairs by the storeroom in back? The door's locked, but there's a key hanging from a leather thong behind a picture of my mom, just to the left."

"Now that sounds really secure," he muttered.

She laughed. "I heard that. But it certainly shows me you've never lived in a small town like Aspen Creek. After you come upstairs, go through my apartment to the kitchen in back. If you could just unlock the French doors, then I can jump down onto the second-floor balcony and get back inside without anyone else—like the whole fire department—learning about my dad's little mistake. Okay?"

He dutifully wound his way through the store, past the glittering chandeliers and stained-glass lamps, old rockers and ornately carved tables glowing in the warm light with the patina of well-loved old age.

With every step he kept an eye out for the fragile doodads parked on every flat surface and hoped he could make it past without knocking anything to the floor.

He expected more of the same—fuss and frills and probably mind-numbing pink ruffles everywhere in Keeley's personal space. Instead the bright and airy upstairs apartment was like the woman herself—welcoming and classy with its cream walls, white wooden blinds and an eclectic mix of antique and modern furnishings that invited rather than overwhelmed.

But while the apartment felt welcoming, his first step out onto the tipsy balcony in back made him shudder.

At the far edge of the tiny platform he could see the top bar of a wrought-iron fire escape dangling toward the ground, but the wood-plank flooring of the balcony showed ample evidence of rot. Reaching that ladder to escape a fire seemed more risky than just going for a two-story leap off the edge.

The rusted wrought-iron fire-escape ladder heading up to the roof looked even worse.

"None of this is safe," he called out to her. "I think I'm going to call 9-1-1 after all."

She peered over the roof edge above him. "No, don't—please. I'm going to just dangle over the edge and drop lightly. It'll be fine."

Maybe until her feet hit the fragile planks and went right through.

"If it's so fine, why didn't you set up a ten-foot ladder on the balcony to get up there in the first place?"

"The contractor said the balcony was still serviceable, but I agree with you. It's one of the next projects on my list."

Connor eyed the spindly railing and weakened floor-boards. "If he thought this was okay, then I'd say he isn't the guy you want to hire. You need someone with more common sense."

"Look—I can handle this on my own, now that you've unlocked the door. I just need you to step back inside so I don't land on you. I'll be careful."

Connor stepped into the doorway, with one foot still on the balcony.

A moment later she slowly backed over the edge of the

roof, her feet dangling a few feet above the floorboards. He grabbed her by the waist and hauled her into the kitchen before she could drop.

Dressed as she was in a heavy gray sweatshirt and faded jeans, she felt surprisingly delicate and light in his arms, and the soft scent of some sort of flowery perfume wafted into the room.

When was the last time he'd inhaled such a wonderful scent? He couldn't remember.

"Ooof!" she exclaimed as he quickly released her and stepped back. "Thanks."

It had been at least six years since he'd held a woman in his arms, and he felt an unaccustomed warmth flowing through him that settled in his chest and robbed him of breath. "Uh…no problem."

"I really do owe you," she murmured, averting her gaze as she dusted her hands against her jeans. A rosy blush brightened her cheeks. "You have no idea how much I wanted to avoid having Todd show up—he's a deputy in town—or the fire-department guys. You can be sure it would've been front-page news in the local paper, complete with photographs. Like I said, I would never live it down. And my dad…"

She closed her eyes briefly, clearly cringing at the thought.

"He's…" Connor hesitated. "Quite a driver."

Her mouth twitched, and then she laughed softly. "That has to be the understatement of the year. But I promise you, I'll be taking his keys away. I won't let him get behind the wheel again and risk someone's life."

The small kitchen, with its white cupboards and yellow-checkered curtains, had seemed as bright and airy as the rest of the apartment, but now he felt the walls closing in on him.

Maybe it was the claustrophobia he'd been fighting since walking out of the prison doors.

Maybe it was his increasing awareness of her sparkling green eyes and her creamy skin, or his sudden curiosity about what it might be like to hold her in his arms just one more time. But that was a *bad* idea.

His ex-wife had provided a painful lesson on the risks of judging women based on beauty, and there was no room in his life for any ties at any rate. The moment his truck was fixed, he needed to be back on the road.

He cleared his throat. "I guess I'd better be going."

He turned for the door to go downstairs, but she touched his arm and he froze at the warmth of her hand.

"Please—wait. Did you find a job in town?"

He knew what she was going to ask, even before she spoke. He shook his head.

"Have you given any more thought to working here?"

He looked over his shoulder, ready to say no and be on his way, but the hope in her eyes stopped him short. "I wouldn't be much use. As soon as my truck's done I need to hit the road, no matter what."

Her expression inexplicably brightened, though how she heard anything positive in his reply escaped him.

"I totally understand, and that's fine. Even a week or two would help. Would you be willing to fill out a job application, just in case you change your mind?"

He swallowed hard, knowing it was only fair to tell her the truth before this went any further. A burning wave of humiliation rushed through him over what he now had to reveal to this pretty young woman—one who had probably never received so much as a parking ticket.

"You really wouldn't want me here."

"Why not?" A teasing glint sparkled in her eyes. "It

isn't like you've just landed on Mars, you know. The store may be slanted to female customers, but the job is easy."

She sure was determined, he'd give her that. He sighed. "There are things you don't know about me, ma'am."

She tossed a grin over her shoulder as she started down the stairs. "Just put it all on the application. You seem like a nice guy, so I'm sure there won't be any problems."

That was what *she* thought.

At the cash-register counter, she handed him another application and a pen, and motioned to the ice-cream table and chair by the front window. "Just have a seat. It won't take long."

Defeated by her perseverance and the ingrained Texas manners that precluded arguing with a lady, he skimmed over the application.

There were four places to list previous employers, and his job history certainly had a suspicious five-year hole in it. What should he write there—inmate? Infirmary worker while incarcerated at the Eagle Creek State Prison in Montana?

The job before that was "rodeo cowboy" and before that he'd been the hardworking son of a Texas rancher. Fixing fences, training horses and raising cattle were hardly good work experiences for the kind of employee she needed.

But the part he'd expected—listing past convictions—wasn't on the form. Maybe times had changed and those details couldn't be asked.

Yet he couldn't lie and he wouldn't hide the truth. He fixed his weary gaze on the glittering baubles hanging over the front counter. "As much as I could use the money, I'm really not your guy."

She tipped her head and smiled at him. "The cash register is super easy, I promise."

He sighed heavily. "Your application form doesn't ask about legal history."

She blinked, clearly not expecting a comment like that, and drew back. "And?"

"It should." He fished in his back pocket for his billfold and withdrew a folded photocopy of a newspaper article, smoothed it out on the counter and then handed it to her. "Read this."

Her mouth dropped open at the headline. She darted a quick look at him then read the brief article he already knew by heart, word for word.

> Texan Connor Rafferty, sentenced to life without parole for the murder of Sheriff Carl Dornan, has served five years in the Eagle Creek State Prison. Recent DNA evidence has exonerated Rafferty of all charges and he has been released. No one else has been charged, but state investigators say the case is ongoing…

"Five years," she breathed, giving him a searching look. "Five years of your life gone and they were *wrong*?"

He'd expected doubt, suspicion, even instant fear of a man she might still believe to be a cop killer despite laboratory evidence to the contrary. He'd expected her to order him out of her store. He hadn't expected to see the sympathy in her eyes.

He hitched a shoulder. "That's about it. But right now I'm just thankful to be free."

"I can't imagine what it was like for you." She shook her head slowly. "And for your poor family."

"Nothing good." He tucked the article back into his wallet. "I don't think you want a guy fresh out of prison at your cash register."

Her brows drew together as she searched his face. "But you weren't guilty, right?"

"No. But I spent five years behind bars and I'll be marked by that injustice forever."

"Maybe you should give people a chance to prove you wrong."

"Is it worth the risk? If word about my past spreads, people might be afraid to come into your store."

"You aren't exactly unique. Marvella Peters is a beautician in town, and one of her nephews in Chicago was released from prison for burglary two years ago. The same situation—based on DNA." She thought for a moment. "And I saw a television show about this sort of thing, too. At least you aren't the poor man who put in *thirty* years before proven innocent."

He'd spent his years in prison knowing he'd never be freed, given the enormity of the charges against him and a federal sentence without chance of parole. A bleak, suffocating sense of hopelessness had weighed on his chest every minute of every day.

God had forgotten him well before his incarceration and he'd given up on prayer long before that. But now he felt a tentative flare of hope and silent words began to form into a rusty, awkward plea. Was it really possible to start over? To be given a chance?

Please, God. Let it be true. But even as he breathed that prayer, he knew it wasn't possible.

His own father had never cared enough to forgive him and offer him another chance, so why would the Almighty?

"I'm really sorry, and I hope you won't be offended, but—" Keeley bit her lower lip. "I—I do need to check out your story. Can I photocopy that article?"

"Of course."

It would be an easy way out for her, once she thought this through a little longer. A delay, followed by a tactful withdrawal of her job offer.

He didn't expect anything more.

Chapter Three

The next day Keeley stopped at the sheriff's office during her lunch break feeling decidedly upbeat. *Finally.* An employee—and one she felt good about hiring. Was God finally answering her prayers and maybe using her to give this man a new start?

It didn't take long to receive a second opinion on Connor Rafferty.

"How much worse could this guy be?" Deputy Todd Hansmann shoved the job application back across his desk and threw up his hands in disgust. "An ex-con? Are you *crazy*?"

Keeley rolled her eyes. His irritable tone confirmed that she'd been right to firmly decline Todd's occasional offers for dinner or a movie when she'd first moved back to Aspen Creek.

Now he was engaged to a take-charge redhead named Nina, who didn't take sass from anyone and who managed the one grocery store in town. They seemed like a perfect match.

"No, I'm not crazy." She stabbed her forefinger at the photocopied newspaper clipping. "If I was, I would've hired him without checking out his story. But I've read about counterfeiters making currency with a computer, so I wanted to make sure this newspaper article wasn't faked. Can you verify this for me?"

He snorted. "Lorraine is running a background check right now. But since he spent five years in the slammer, there must have been some mighty compelling evidence to lock him up in the first place. If he got released on some technicality—"

"DNA is not a technicality. It's *proof.* Right?"

"But he got *arrested*, Keel. The cops must have had good reason to be suspicious. If he was just some innocent, random guy, why did they ever consider him? Maybe he has a long history of being a troublemaker."

"*Exonerated*, it says," Keeley repeated, her light mood dissipating.

"That aside, prison changes a man, Keel. And not for the better. I still think—" At the buzz of the intercom on his desk, Todd pushed his chair back. "Just hold on a minute."

Five minutes later he was back with several pages of printouts in hand, his mouth twisted into an unpleasant grimace. "Lorraine finished the background check. Apparently his story is true."

"So someone in law enforcement was careless and he paid for their mistakes?"

"There were DNA errors, apparently. His legal record has been wiped clean. Uh… Lorraine even found some articles about the case and his release through the National Registry of Exonerations."

A feeling of jubilation bubbled up in Keeley's chest. "I told you!"

"You still shouldn't take any chances."

"*Really*, Todd."

"Think about the kind of prisoners he's been associating

with…and about that last new employee of yours. Mandy. Candy—whatever her name was."

"Mindy. I hardly think this guy would abscond with froufrou from the store."

Todd's eyes narrowed on her. "No, but he might run off with the cash register. Does your brother know about this? Your sister?"

They'd all gone to elementary through high school together here in town, so he knew her siblings well enough to track them down and give each a call.

Brad, a doctor in Cleveland, and Liza, a tax attorney in St. Paul, would have plenty to say if they learned of Keeley's plans, and knowing Todd, they would probably be finding out all too soon.

She tried to hold back her rising irritation. "Why would this matter to them? They aren't partners in my store, Todd. I don't answer to anyone but myself."

"Still—"

"I appreciate your concern, but this is my decision." She reached across the counter and gave his hand a squeeze. "Thanks for the background check."

He glowered at her. "So you're going to hire a felon."

She bit back a sharp retort and summoned a more reasonable tone. "Is he still a felon if proved innocent via irrefutable proof?"

She'd come here to make sure Connor's story was true. That accomplished, it was time to leave before she said something she would regret. "I was really happy to hear about your engagement, by the way. Say hi to Nina for me, okay?"

Todd waved away the pleasantries and made a sound of disgust deep in his throat. "Did you know that they've never found another suspect for that murder? *None?* I hope that makes you think twice."

* * *

Keeley left the sheriff's office fuming at Todd's unwavering opinion about her lack of common sense.

But with the help of a hot dog plus a large Heath Bar Blizzard for lunch at the Dairy Queen, followed by a fast-paced, twenty-minute walk, she'd calmed down enough to realize that she at least owed it to herself to check out Connor's story a little further.

Maybe she *was* a tad impetuous at times—not that she'd admit it to Todd or her father—and she often led with her heart instead of her head when it came to assessing people and their intentions. But was that so wrong?

Maybe at times, as evidenced by the last three clerks she'd hired. And if she were honest with herself, she had to admit that she could understand Todd's concern.

She'd been stunned when Connor walked into her shop moments after she'd recklessly promised God—in *prayer*, which surely must be binding—that she'd trust Him and would offer a job to the next person who walked into her store.

But she'd expected a nicely dressed middle-aged woman to come in the door—her usual sort of clientele—not a tall, lean cowboy whose handsome, chiseled face belonged on a hero in a Western movie. And she hadn't exactly expected he'd be fresh out of prison, either—no matter what the circumstances of his incarceration. Had Connor been *completely* honest with her?

She'd felt a shiver of instant attraction when he'd come into her store, and when he'd briefly held her in his arms while helping her down from the roof, her pulse had kicked into overdrive and her stomach had fluttered. She'd felt the warmth of an embarrassing blush rise to her face.

But whatever her foolish reaction might have been to this stranger, she would be stupid not to check out his story even further. His thick black hair, silvery blue eyes and strong jaw might be compelling, but that didn't mean he was trustworthy.

Keeley got back in her car and drove slowly past Red's Mechanic Shop & Wrecker Service. The three garage doors were all open, revealing a trio of SUVs in the service bays.

Her heart dropped. Just as she'd feared, there wasn't a pickup in sight. Had Connor lied about the reason he was in town?

Maybe he'd just been casing her store…

At that thought, she had to laugh.

With her current financial state, there would be little cash to steal, and what interest could he possibly have in costume jewelry, local artists and pretty little antiques?

She turned around, pulled into the parking area and went looking for Red. He was sitting with his feet propped up at his desk in the cramped office, his thick fingers stained black with grease and motor oil, eating a sandwich.

He waved her toward a chair filled with a haphazard stack of invoices. "So how's that New Yorker running, missy?"

At thirty-one, she was still "missy" to the man who had been fixing her dad's cars for forty years. She smiled. "Like a clock. You do great work."

"It ought to last another hundred thousand, but I'm not so sure about your dad, though."

"That he'll last that long?"

"That he oughta drive that long. I hear he had a little trouble yesterday afternoon."

She fidgeted with her keys. "Oh?"

"Millie Ferguson was closing up her shop and saw him make some pretty strange moves on Main."

Keeley groaned. Knitting Pretty was across the street from her own shop and just a couple of doors down. Its bay windows offered Millie a stellar view of everything happening on Main. She never missed a thing, and she never hesitated to share it.

"How did you hear about that?"

"At the coffee shop this morning. Good thing no one else was on the street."

"Did…she say anything else?"

He chuckled. "Only that she saw a handsome cowboy talking to you yesterday. And she said she's gonna keep a sharp eye out for your dad's car and stay out of his way."

If Dad's little accident was already fodder for the coffee-shop crowd, then the whole town knew. "I just hope no one razzes him about it."

"I imagine they will. No doubt about it." He took another bite and continued talking around the mouthful. "So what can I do for you?"

Well, *this* was awkward. "I, um… Nothing, really. I heard you towed in a pickup yesterday."

He lowered the sandwich and winked. "The cowboy. Is he a close friend of yours, by any chance?"

She could see the Aspen Creek gossip mill churning if she didn't make things perfectly clear. "Actually, he might work at my store for a couple weeks while he's waiting for his truck. But I was just driving by and didn't see it on any of your lifts."

"It's parked out back."

Relief washed through her. "Thanks."

"I'll get to it as soon as I can. But maybe you'll want him to stick around longer." Red grinned and reached over to give her a pat on the shoulder with a beefy paw. "I've never been one to stand in the way of true love, you know."

She cringed at the way he warbled out the last words.

Red had always liked to tease her whenever she'd stopped here with Dad as a little girl. Now she wished she hadn't come by to snoop. "Nothing of the kind," she said firmly. "He's just a potential employee."

Red gave her a knowing look as he took another bite of his sandwich. "Whatever you say, darlin'. Whatever you say."

That meant the diner crowd would likely be hearing another chapter of her life the next time Red stopped in for his favorite rhubarb pie.

She was just climbing into her Honda SUV when Red came to the open door of his shop. "Your cowboy stopped by just an hour ago and fetched the rest of his camping gear from the back of his truck. If you need to find him, check out the Aspen Creek Campgrounds. But keep an eye on the weather, honey. Looks like more storms are rolling in."

"Thanks, Red." Turning for Dad's two-story brick house on Cedar, she flipped on the radio and mulled her options as she drove through town. *Okay, Lord. Unless You give me a big sign, I'm going to give that cowboy another chance to say yes.*

As she pulled to a stop in front of her father's house, her heart fell. "*Dad?* What on earth...?"

She shouldered on her Marmot rain jacket and hurried up the cement walk leading to his front porch, where Paul North sat on the porch swing in a wet short-sleeved shirt, huddled into himself and obviously chilled to the bone. "You'll catch pneumonia out here. Why aren't you inside?"

He shot an irritable glance at her. "Bart."

"The *dog*?" She glanced around the empty front yard. "Where is he?"

He hiked a thumb toward the house. "He must've jumped against the door and shut it while I was getting my mail."

Right. She shut her eyes briefly at the thought of her elderly father walking the two blocks to the post office then losing his keys. "You went in the rain? Without a jacket?"

"It wasn't raining when I left," he snapped.

"This is important, Dad. What if I hadn't stopped by? What if it was colder outside? You could end up in the hospital." She fingered through her keys and unlocked the heavy oak front door. "Do you remember where we put your extra keys after the last time you got locked out?"

"Of course I do. They're gone."

She went to the farthest brick pillar supporting the porch roof, felt for the single loose brick, retrieved the slim metal box behind it and held it up for him to see. "Right in here, Dad."

He gave her hand a blank look then shrugged. "Then you didn't put them back right the last time. Too far back."

Stifling an exasperated sigh, she held the door open for him and ushered him inside. He'd locked himself out before—without the unlikely help of his crotchety, lazy old dog—hence the keys hidden at both the front and back doors. He was just seventy-three, but now the trick was for him to remember where they were.

One more sign that his independence was fading and her responsibility for him had to increase—despite his stubborn refusal. "You need one of those medical alert necklaces, Dad. Push a button and help is on the way."

He visibly shuddered. "Over my dead, cold body."

"Or if you'd just put your cell phone in your pocket every morning and keep it there, you could call for help if you locked yourself out or fell—"

"I'm not an invalid," he growled as he shuffled across the kitchen to the central hallway and the staircase leading to the second-floor bedrooms. "I'm going up to take a hot shower."

Frustration welled up in her chest as she watched him disappear down the hall. She stopped by as often as she could and never knew what she might find. "I'll be back in an hour and make some supper, okay?" she called out to him.

"Suit yourself." A few minutes later she heard the distant slam of his bedroom door.

Even on his best days he could be short-tempered—especially if anything occurred to highlight his lapses in memory or judgment. She understood that he feared the eventual loss of his independence, she really did.

But still.

Was it too much to expect a bit of kindness from him when she tried to help? He often seemed to think she was an enemy now. She sighed heavily as she looked heavenward and prayed for patience.

I'm trying my best, God. Please—just give me strength and help me keep him safe.

She touched the local weather app on her iPhone, glanced at yet another line of approaching rain on the Doppler radar screen and hurried to her car.

There'd been no responses to her Help Wanted ad in the paper today, so she would try to find Connor, ask him one last time and pray he would agree.

It was probably a waste of time trying to track down someone who didn't want to work for her. Once again, he was going to refuse.

But with just seven days until the biggest tourist weekend of the year, what were the chances of finding anyone else in time?

With rain falling yet again, starting a campfire was hopeless. Connor grabbed his shaving kit, a towel and change of clothes, and headed for the two-sided, concrete-block pavilion that offered shade and shelter for a dozen picnic tables, with restrooms and shower facilities in the attached building behind.

He settled on one of the picnic tables under the dim illumination of a hanging lightbulb and pulled out an old Lee Child novel from his kit. But his thoughts kept wandering and he finally tossed the book aside to stare out at the rain as his memories flooded back.

Josh in his fuzzy purple pajamas, laughing as he raced around the house to avoid story time because that meant bedtime. Making motor noises as he played with his tractors, pretending he was plowing the carpet.

The fresh, clean scent of him after bath time, his cheeks rosy and his dark, wet hair standing up in spikes that made him imagine he was a dinosaur.

He'd been four then; would he remember any of those days? Anything at all? Or would he be frightened when he saw Connor again for the first time in years? *If I can get you back, you're going to have a safe, happy life, little cowboy—I promise you that.*

The boy's life sure hadn't started that way.

The marriage had been troubled from the beginning, starting with the cute buckle bunny who'd swept Connor off his feet. He had never regretted Joshua's arrival—not for a second. But the shotgun marriage was something he and Marsha had both come to regret.

They'd been just twenty-one. He'd had to follow the rodeo circuit, while she'd resented being trapped at home with an unplanned baby. Their initial mutual infatuation had quickly dimmed.

But Connor hadn't wanted a divorce. He'd prayed that he and Marsha could find some calm middle ground—maybe even come to love each other—to give their child a stable, peaceful home.

Just more prayers that God hadn't seen fit to answer.

During his last year in prison, he'd tried attending Bible study for a while, needing something—*anything*—that could give him answers and a sense of peace about his past in the midst of the desolation he'd felt over his incarceration. He hadn't found the answers he'd wanted.

Hard-hearted, just like your dad.

The words came out of nowhere—as loud and clear as if the accusation had been spoken inside his head.

And with them came an onslaught of bitter memories.

Chris and Dan had been the hardworking sons, the ones who'd managed to get along with Dad, while Connor had been the rebel who'd bucked authority and refused to bend.

His teen years had been pure misery…except for competing in high-school rodeo. That had been the ticket to send Connor off on the college circuit…then into the pros after graduation.

Dad had been furious, but rodeo was Connor's life. All he'd ever wanted to do, and he'd never looked back.

Dad's disgust when Connor had called home to tell him about the baby and his sudden marriage had sealed the deal. There'd been no more phone calls from anyone at the ranch after that. Josh had never even met his uncles and grandfather.

What kind of man showed no interest in his grandson? He hadn't even bothered to show up at Connor's murder trial a few states away, either. As far as Connor knew, no one at the ranch had ever checked on the outcome…and Connor had been too proud to write.

Even as his old anger and hurt started to simmer, that same inner voice told Connor exactly what he didn't want to hear.

It's not only Dad's fault. A bigger man would go back and apologize for the pain he'd caused.

Connor turned his cell phone over in his hand, wondering what he'd hear if he called the ranch after all these years.

Probably just the old man slamming the receiver down once more.

Why give him that chance?

Connor shoved his cell into the back pocket of his jeans and headed for the camp shower building…though his inner voice refused to stay quiet.

But what about Josh—doesn't he deserve to know his grandpa? His uncles? If you wait too long, someday it will be too late.

A mile out of town Keeley turned off the highway onto the long gravel road leading to the Aspen Creek Campgrounds. She pulled to a stop by the concrete-block picnic pavilion overlooking the creek and surveyed the nearly deserted campsites.

Two pop-up camping trailers were barely visible through the trees. A 1970s motor home stood parked at the far end of the central clearing with no sign of any inhabitants. There were no tents, and no wonder, with the heavy storms that had been sweeping through the county since last night. Even now, raindrops were pattering on the roof of her car and a distant flash of lightning pierced the dense forest to the west.

This was a lovely campground—typical for this part of Wisconsin—but anyone with common sense would opt out of tent camping during weather like this.

She drummed her fingertips on the steering wheel. Had Connor chosen a more isolated spot somewhere else in the heavily wooded, hundred-acre park? If so, the possibility of finding him was almost nil now that ominous clouds hid the early evening sun, turning the landscape to deepening shades of gray.

Shifting her car into Drive, she started forward. Then slammed on the brakes.

She felt a little shiver of awareness even before Connor rounded the back of the building wearing a long, cowboy-style oilskin raincoat, a towel flung over his shoulder and a shaving kit dangling from his fingertips. The overhead security lights gave her a good glimpse of his face before he turned and sauntered toward the campsites along the creek. He didn't glance in her direction.

Her heart gave an extra thud—yet again—and she inhaled a shaky breath. *Oh, my.*

Now he was clean-shaven, his wet hair slicked back. But it wasn't just that he looked like some broad-shouldered, hard-edged heartthrob—she'd learned her lesson long ago about how little a handsome face mattered over the long haul. It was something far deeper that drew her.

The pain and sorrow she'd seen in his eyes.

His stubborn honesty about his past.

And the way he'd come to her rescue like some cowboy in an old Western movie, by circling her waist with his strong, capable hands and helping her off the roof...then breaking the awkward moment afterward with a disarming flash of humor.

She saw him moving at a faster clip toward the pines along the creek bank, and if she didn't gather her thoughts, she was going to lose him.

She rolled down her window. "Hey, cowboy!"

He turned in surprise and waited as she drove up beside him.

"Nice night for camping," she said with a smile.

"As long as the wind stays down." A corner of his mouth kicked up as he glanced toward the black, roiling clouds rapidly building over the treetops to the west. "What brings you way out here?"

"I think you know," she said dryly.

He studied her for a long moment then sighed. "You checked out my story."

She nodded, feeling her cheeks warm. "I have an old friend at the sheriff's office, and he got right on it."

Connor stilled. "And?"

"I really do need help now. When the college kids come back for summer break, I can probably hire one of them for the tourist season, but—"

"All right."

"Though that's six weeks away and by then you'll be long gone anyway, so—" She faltered to a stop and stared at him. "Wait a minute. You'll do it?"

"You were right. I could use the cash, so if you need help, I'm game." He gave the sky another glance. "If this weather keeps up, I might need to pay for a place to stay that actually has a roof."

Relief washed through her. "I open at ten on Saturdays, so can you come in tomorrow—say, nine o'clock? I could pick you up."

"No need." The soft rain intensified and he pulled up the hood of his coat. "I just hope you don't come to regret this. You might if folks find out about who you just hired."

Chapter Four

"So as you can see, this cash register is really easy." Keeley gave the drawer a firm shove to close it. "Any questions?"

"Nope." But the store, with its thousands of frilly, sparkly, dangly things everywhere and the multitude of stained-glass lamps hanging from the ceiling, made him want to go rope a steer. Bale hay. *Anything* that would be outside and far from town, where a man could drag in a deep breath and not inhale the scents of soaps and fancy creams and a forest of dried flower arrangements.

Why anyone would want a bunch of dead flowers instead of fresh ones, he couldn't even begin to fathom. He rubbed the back of his neck.

"I can tell you're really loving this," she said dryly. "So let's get on with the tour, okay?"

He nodded and followed her into the storeroom, where deep shelving lined each wall from floor to ceiling. A worktable held a coffeemaker, gift wrap and a pile of shipping supplies. "I don't suppose you've done much gift wrapping and shipping."

"Nope." He thought back over the difficult four years of his marriage. He'd hung in there, trying to make his son's life normal and happy, but there hadn't been much to celebrate with a wife who'd often met her girlfriends in bars, drank too much and didn't always come home.

"Wrapping is easy." She collected two gift boxes from the shelf over the table and pulled two lengths of bright pink paper from one of the rollers, then handed him a tape dispenser and scissors. "Just copy what I do, step by step."

She led him through the process three times before she was satisfied, then showed him how to affix a Keeley's Antiques & Gifts sticker and a bow on the top. "Easy, right?"

Bows and sparkly pink wrapping paper. What would his brothers think of him now? He thought longingly about *stacking* hay. Cleaning horse stalls. Wrestling calves for branding. "Uh…right."

No wonder she'd seemed hesitant—even wary—when she'd first offered him a job. Desperate as she was to find help, even she must have seen that he wouldn't be good at this.

"The shipping boxes are all stacked flat, but are super easy to make up." She reached for one on an upper shelf and whipped it together in the blink of an eye. "You can use crumpled paper or the little air-filled cushioning pillows—in that box over there. No foam packing peanuts. I *hate* those peanuts."

"What about sweeping around here? Mowing—and those maintenance projects you mentioned? I'd be better at that."

"Yes, but you aren't getting off that easy."

Her eyes twinkled. "If I need to leave to check on my dad or need to run to an estate auction, for instance, I'll need you to handle things here. I've already got a boy who comes to sweep and such after school. You'll meet Bobby on Monday."

He caught a flash of movement above head level to his left and spun around, expecting to catch something falling from a shelf.

A scrawny white cat glared down at him, its back arched and tail raised. With a torn ear and one eye closed, it looked like a pirate fallen on bad times. Its superior expression suggested that it knew Connor wasn't much better off.

"Rags," Keeley murmured as she deftly finished preparing and sealing another shipping box. "Any questions?"

"Rags?"

"The cat."

"It looks…" He was at a loss for words. Maybe it was her prized possession, but it was the homeliest creature he'd ever seen.

"Worse for wear?" She smiled up at the furry beast, then reached into a dorm-size refrigerator under the counter, grabbed a can of cat food and pulled back the tab on the lid. She set it on the workbench. "He showed up a few weeks ago and I didn't have the heart to turn him away. He's never let me touch him, but I'm working on it. Once we're friends, I'll catch him and get him vaccinated and neutered."

"I'm sure he'll love that," Connor said dryly.

"Not his choice, given the feral-cat population around here." She put the shipping materials away then turned to face Connor once more. "So—this is where my extra stock is. I've labeled the larger boxes clearly, and small items are in labeled plastic totes. If I'm not here and you have any questions, there's a phone by the register and you can always call my cell."

"I think I can handle it."

She frowned. "Do you have a cell phone? In case I need to reach you?"

"Just a basic no-contract, prepaid phone I picked up in Montana. Text and calls, but no internet."

"That works." She reached for her back jeans' pocket, took out her phone and punched in his number as he recited it to her, then gave him her number. "We're all set, then."

"You mentioned repairs." He gestured toward a five-gallon pail strategically placed under a slowly dripping leak in the ceiling by the back wall. "Do you have a list?"

At that she rolled her eyes. "Sadly, more lists than I could keep track of. I finally had to start putting them all in a ring notebook along with a raft of estimates. Most of the jobs are big and will require more time than you'll be here, or need to be done by someone licensed and bonded. I've got all that scheduled. But there are endless small jobs, believe me."

"How long have you been here?"

"Three years. I've already done quite a bit to this place, but the building is older than a lot of my antiques, and it was empty for several years before I bought it. The repairs and updates just don't end—and now I have a ticking clock, as it were."

He moved to the window facing the alley and ran a hand over the water damage on the sill. "A deadline?"

A faint blush rose in her cheeks. "I've had a few financial problems and now I need to refinance a short-term reno loan within a couple months, plus my mortgage while the rates are still low."

"Seems like this is a successful business, though."

"Depends. Tourism plummeted last year due to a cold, wet spring and blistering-hot, humid summer. It was like a ghost town during our busy season. Not only that, but last year I had to replace the furnace and AC, and this year all of the plumbing. My dad still insists that I was a fool to buy this building, but I'm going to prove him wrong." She heaved a sigh. "I hope."

Connor whistled. "Bad year."

She nodded. "The loan officer says he won't refinance if the place isn't fully up to code, and he'll require a full inspection. There's a lot of work left to do."

"There must be contractors around here, though."

"Some, but the best one is booked six months out. I've been on his schedule since February, for a number of projects." She eyed him thoughtfully. "Your job application listed past jobs as ranching and rodeo. I guess I don't exactly know what your skills are."

He laughed. "Not many that apply to this place."

"So, you grew up on a ranch?"

"Yep. We raised cattle, horses and hay. But then a bad case of 'bright lights and big city' knocked me sideways. After graduating from college I ended up on the pro rodeo circuit for nine years."

She tilted her head and studied him for a moment. "Can you go back to rodeo now?"

"I've been away too long, and championship-level rodeo is mostly a younger man's sport, except something like team roping. Eventually I would've needed to stop and do something else anyway."

"Like what?"

He gave a self-deprecating laugh. "That will take serious thought."

"What about going back to your family's ranch?"

He ignored the twinge of pain in his heart whenever he thought about the angry phone conversations with his dad during his first few years away from home—calls that had always ended with Dad slamming the phone into its cradle.

"Nope. That water went down the creek long time ago. As the oldest son, I was expected to head home after college and eventually take over, not go all over the country chasing dreams. My dad quit talking to me years ago."

She reached out and rested a hand on his arm—a gesture that sent a warm rush of sensation straight to his chest. "I'm so sorry."

"My incarceration sealed that deal anyway, but it's all right. I'm thirty-three and it's not too late to go back to grad school or vet school. That was my plan in the first place once I'd saved enough winnings on the rodeo circuit."

Her brows drew together. "But still…it's your *family*, Connor. Do you have any brothers or sisters? What about your mom?"

"Mom walked out on Dad while I was in high school and moved out East. She never came back. My younger brothers were bitter when I took off, because they were left behind to work on the ranch. But now they manage the whole spread, so they've got a good deal going." He shrugged. "When I've got my future sorted out again, I'll give them a call. But not before."

She searched his face, her eyes filled with sympathy. "At least you're free now and can get on with your life. Right?"

He nodded. It had been years since he'd held a hammer, but maybe working here could give him a current reference for when he started job hunting, after he'd dealt with Marsha in Detroit.

For the first time, he felt a glimmer of hope.

"I don't know which of our dads is the bigger challenge," she said with a rueful shake of her head. "Mine used to be a general contractor. Just six months ago he was helping with the reno projects around here, but now his mind is failing and he's more testy than ever. You never know what's ahead in life, right?"

He almost laughed at that.

One day he'd been climbing into his pickup to reach the next rodeo up in Butte—the next he'd been behind bars and accused of murder.

And nothing—not his prayers to the God who no longer cared, not his lawyer and not even a witness who'd seen him that night elsewhere—had made one bit of difference.

Chapter Five

At five o'clock Keeley flipped the sign in the front window to Closed and peered out at cars driving past, windshield wipers on high. Thunder rumbled again, making the wood flooring beneath her feet vibrate.

"I cannot believe this is the third rainy day in a row. The forecasters say it's a 'stalled front.' I'm just praying it decides to pack up and move on tomorrow."

Connor came out of the back room, his Western-style oilskin coat draped over his arm. "Why then?"

"The Antique Walk starts Friday."

"You've mentioned it before, but I'm still not sure what it involves."

"There's usually a big flea market at the fairgrounds, with a carnival and rides, but everything could end up a big, muddy mess if the ground doesn't dry out first."

"Sounds like quite an event."

"It's supposed to be. Several of the churches put up food tents, the 4-H clubs set up a petting zoo and the FFA—Future Farmers of America—club coordinates a tractor pull and a horse show. The quilters raffle some beautiful quilts for charity—the list goes on and on." She bustled around the store, pulling down the window shades facing the sidewalk and adjusting the positioning of the merchandise. "But it only works out well if the weather is nice and we get the big crowds from Minneapolis and Chicago."

She moved to the cash register and began counting the money into neat stacks, tallied the total and slipped the money into a zippered bank deposit bag to drop off on the way home.

"Last spring was cold and windy, so we had the smallest crowd in years. We ended up in the red on event costs and didn't reach our donation goals for heart disease and cancer research, either."

Connor walked to the front door and studied the sign displaying the store hours. "So, your store is open tomorrow afternoon?"

She nodded, dropped the bank deposit bag into her purse and grabbed her car keys from a drawer under the counter. "All of the stores in town are open Sunday afternoons. Weekends are the busiest times during high season, and none of us can afford to close for the entire day, even if we want to. It would really decimate the weekend traffic coming from the big cities."

"So, do you want me to come in tomorrow?" He shouldered on his coat.

"I'd like you here every day, if possible. Your time in town will be short as it is." She smiled. "You've caught on really fast and your help means more to me than you'll ever know."

"The more hours, the better. Noon, then?"

"Perfect." She eyed the light rain outside. "How on earth do you start a campfire when it's this wet?"

"Can't."

"Then how will you cook your supper? Do you have a propane gas stove or something?"

"Something like that." Thunder rumbled again as he opened the door to step outside. "G'night."

"Wait." Guilt lanced through her at the thought of him heading out into the rain. She slung her purse over her shoulder and hurried after him. "I'm definitely giving you a ride home tonight."

He turned to face her, the rain sluicing down his coat. "I don't mind the walk at all, ma'am."

"I just had an idea. I'm heading over to Dad's house to make supper and I'd like you to come along."

"That isn't necessary. Really."

She waved away his protest. "Consider it a part of your workday, because this will help me a lot, as well. You can talk to Dad while I make supper and then you can eat with us. I am sure there'll be a time or two when I need to send you over there, so it'll help if he gets to know you. Maybe not anything about your, um, recent past, though. Not just yet."

Frowning, he hitched a shoulder as if wanting to turn her down. "Well…"

She bit her lower lip. "I want to apologize in advance for anything Dad might say or do that seems rude. He wasn't always that way. His doctor says it's probably part of his dementia."

A corner of Connor's mouth kicked up into a brief grin. "Actually, it sounds just like home."

Not for the first time, she wondered about what Connor's life had been like before he'd ended up in prison.

Not always happy, apparently, from his hints about his troubled family life back at the ranch. Yet he'd been nothing but polite, with the subtle undercurrent of Texas charm that made her heart warm. Whatever he'd suffered during his unjust incarceration, he'd still managed to come through it as a kind and decent man. "So you'll join us?"

He hesitated, then nodded.

This was strictly business—a way to help introduce Dad to this stranger. So why did she feel such a flicker of delight at his answer?

Connor would be leaving town in no time. She'd never see him again. And she'd already had too many lessons in the art of failed relationships to ever risk her heart again.

She would not—*could* not—have any personal interest in Connor Rafferty.

He raised an eyebrow and she realized she'd been staring at him while sorting out her thoughts. She scrambled for something else to say.

"Um, just steer clear of Dad's dog and you'll be fine."

"I think I'll manage…though it sounds like your dad might be the bigger challenge."

She bit back a laugh. "I forgot. You had a career riding bulls or broncs or something equally intimidating. Right?"

"Saddle broncs."

"So you can easily deal with a grumpy dog." She ushered Connor out the back door of the shop and then locked the door behind them. "I've had a five-pound pot roast in Dad's Crock-Pot since this morning, simmering away with plenty of fresh vegetables and garlic. I hope you'll enjoy it more than a soggy campground and cold food."

He flashed a smile that warmed her clear down to her toes. "On that score, I have no doubt."

Once he'd heard about that beef roast, it would have taken a herd of stampeding Herefords to keep him from joining Keeley and her dad for dinner.

But now that they'd been at her dad's house for an interminable hour, Connor wished he could tactfully leave despite the otherworldly aromas wafting into the family room from the kitchen.

Paul North sat in his La-Z-Boy recliner, his arms folded tightly across his chest.

He'd said nothing when Keeley introduced the two of them, and his icy demeanor hadn't wavered since. Now and then he directed a glare in Connor's direction.

If eyes could shoot flames, Connor would have been a pile of cinders by now. He shifted his weight on the leather sofa and tried another topic. "So…are you a sports fan?"

"No."

Connor had never followed sports, so that would've been a dead end anyhow. "Golf?"

"No."

"Camping? Hiking?"

Paul's thick, steel-gray brows drew together in a frown. "Do I *look* like someone who would go camping?"

Connor glanced around the spacious room. Paneled in dark wood and cluttered with twice as much heavy furniture as it needed, and stacks of magazines on every flat surface, the room was so full that he'd even missed noticing the fireplace at first.

Toenails clicked on the hardwood floor and a white-muzzled, overweight dog appeared at the end of the sofa. It swiveled its head toward Paul then took a long, hard look at Connor, its teeth bared and hackles raised.

The dog and Paul had such similar personalities that Connor nearly laughed. "Nice dog."

"Be careful. Bart doesn't like anyone but me." From the tone in his voice, Paul was proud of it, too.

But just then Bart ambled over to Connor, sniffed at the hem of his jeans, gave a sigh of contentment and planted his rear on the floor.

Connor reached down to ruffle the shaggy hair on his neck and scratch behind his ears. The old dog flopped down to rest his chin on Connor's running shoe. In seconds he was snoring, his flaccid cheeks whuffling in and out with each wheezy breath.

Paul eyed his traitorous dog, and the old man's bushy eyebrows lowered. "I guess *he* thinks you're okay," he muttered.

"Have you had him long?"

"Twelve years. He was a rescue from the animal shelter. No one wanted him till I came along, and we've been pals ever since." A glimmer of a smile appeared briefly at the memory. "You have dogs?"

"I did, when I was still on my dad's ranch in Texas. It was a long time ago."

"A ranch?" Paul's aloof expression faded. "I thought maybe you were some tramp."

From the kitchen came the sound of a strangled laugh, and Keeley peered around the corner of the door. "Dad—for heaven's sake. I told you he's *camping* while his truck is being repaired. That doesn't make him a hobo."

When she disappeared back into the kitchen, Paul gave him a narrowed look. "A *real* ranch?"

Connor nodded, relieved to finally find some common ground. "Real. Horses. Cattle mostly. Around four hundred acres of hay."

"I read a lot of Westerns. Seems like a great life, out there with the wide-open spaces. Clean air."

"That's what I miss most. But it's a hard life and a lonely one at times."

The rich aroma of beef roast grew stronger now, coupled with the scent of biscuits and something that smelled suspiciously like apple pie.

Homemade apple pie? The very thought made Connor's mouth water and stomach rumble. The food had been okay in prison, as far as institutional cooking went, but he could already tell that this meal would be unbelievably good. "I'm guessing your daughter is a very good cook."

"She'll do."

"I heard that, Dad," Keeley teased from the kitchen. "So beef pot roast for Connor but bread and water for you."

Paul ignored her. "Now, my wife, Frances—there was a woman who could cook. She could make magic happen in the kitchen." Paul settled back in his chair, his eyes closing as he drifted back through his memories. "Flakiest piecrusts and fluffiest biscuits you ever tasted. And her fried chicken? Whoo-eee. She could make a man almost cry, just by promising to make it for supper."

Once again Keeley appeared at the door to the kitchen with a pot holder and a smile. "What Dad said is all true. Mom was a wonderful cook. Even using her recipe files, I can't measure up."

Connor's estimation of Keeley moved up another notch.

Apparently the old man didn't appreciate how much his daughter helped him, and he certainly didn't consider his words before speaking. Yet she remained consistently kind, handling him with grace and a touch of humor. Traits so far removed from the party girl he'd married that he couldn't even begin to compare them.

He could only hope that Marsha had matured during the time he'd been in prison. That she'd become a better mom, a stronger person...and that her latest conquest was a man who was good to their son. Shaking off his thoughts, he turned to Paul. "I'm sorry about your loss."

Paul's eyes opened and his smile faded as he came back into the present. "It's been a long time. Fifteen years and four months."

"It must have been hard, losing your wife so young."

"Car accident. All three kids were in the car with her, but only she died." Paul stood slowly, as if favoring a multitude of arthritic joints. "She took my heart with her to the grave, and then I had to raise those kids on my own. Hardest thing I ever did."

At least he'd had the privilege of raising them, though from his sour expression he'd considered it far more work than joy.

Joshua's face flashed into Connor's thoughts and he felt a familiar stab of sorrow over the years he'd lost with his son. The deep longing hit him like a heavy ache in his heart.

How could Paul not see what a blessing he'd been given?

Chapter Six

With a sense of wonder, Keeley watched her dad converse with Connor over dinner about ranching and cowboys and the Old West.

Most days he said only a few words to her, and most of them were orders or complaints. But tonight he seemed to have slipped back to the man he'd been before Mom's death—a sociable man she only vaguely remembered.

It wasn't always easy to keep a conversation going—especially in the face of Dad's irascible personality. If she'd known Connor better, she would've given him a big hug for making such an effort.

Connor looked up after his last bite of apple pie à la mode and grinned at her. "This meal was amazing."

"Thanks. I'm just glad you could come." She looked over at her father, who was already heading to his favorite chair in the living room, and lowered her voice. "I think Dad really enjoyed some male conversation over dinner. Can I bring some coffee into the living room for you?"

"I'd rather help you clean up." He stood and gathered some of the dishes and then followed her into the kitchen.

"Thanks for the offer, but I've already got the prep dishes in the dishwasher, and I'll just load the rest when the first batch is done. You really were a hit, by the way. Both Dad and Bart like you, and that's like hitting a home run around here."

He looked out the double windows over the sink. "He has a beautiful place. It must be hard keeping it all up."

She joined him at the windows. "The flower gardens were incredible when my mom was living. Now it's more like survival of the fittest out there. But Dad putters in the gardens and I do the mowing."

He looked at her with a glint of admiration in his eyes. "No wonder you needed help at the store."

"And you agreed—for which I am deeply thankful." She pointed toward a row of pine trees at the back of the property. "See the three cute cabins out back? My mom had a small B-and-B business going, mostly because she enjoyed the guests. After she died, we eventually had to stop once Dad wasn't up to managing them anymore. It was a nice way to remember Mom, though. I still miss her, even after all these years." Embarrassed that Dad had been so blunt—once again—she felt a warm blush climb to her cheeks. "I'm really sorry about that awkward moment back in the living room. Dad doesn't have much of a filter anymore."

"How did the accident happen?"

"I was barely sixteen, a kid who still assumed we'd all live forever and everything would always be the same. We were on our way to the church Christmas pageant and my younger sister and brother were bickering nonstop in the backseat. I should've turned around and done something to stop the fighting, but I was so entranced by what I was reading that I wasn't paying attention. Mom looked over her shoulder to tell them to be quiet and didn't see the drunk driver who ran a red light. He broadsided our car." Keeley drew in a shaky breath. "She would have had time to avoid him, if she hadn't been distracted."

"Oh, Keeley. I'm so sorry about your loss."

Keeley struggled to regain her train of thought, then closed her eyes briefly as the memory of the accident flooded back in minute and graphic detail, just like an old movie. The one that had played through her brain for years after that terrible day.

"At the funeral we kids overheard Dad telling relatives that the wreck was our fault because we were misbehaving in the car. Believe me, that made our loss a thousand times worse."

"But you were just being kids. She was the one responsible for watching the road. It was an *accident*," Connor murmured. "To say something so cruel, your dad must have been too distraught to even think straight. After the funeral he probably didn't even remember saying it."

The deep compassion in Connor's voice offered her comfort. Peace. And a moment of grace she hadn't ever realized she needed.

"I—I guess I never thought of it that way." She turned away and stared blindly out the window. "I can't tell you how often I considered ending my life during that first year. It was horrible to realize I would never get past that crushing grief because nothing would ever change. How could it? Mom would never come back. Life would never again be like it was. And the ragged hole in my heart would never heal. I knew I would feel guilty forever."

"But…it got better."

"Yeah. I used to hate the people who told me 'time heals all wounds.' I *hated* that they dared minimize my grief. But…I guess they were right." She gave him a watery smile. "Sorry—I don't usually trap people into hearing all of that."

His beautiful eyes filled with deep understanding and he smiled gently. "I'm so sorry about all you went through."

Feeling awkward and unbalanced after revealing so

much of herself, she stole a glance at her watch. "Oh, gosh. It's getting late. I want to give you a ride home, but I need to talk to Dad for a minute. Okay?"

"I can walk back on my own."

"No, I'll drive you. It's not a problem at all, because I have to drive home anyway. If you want to go on out, I'll meet you at the car."

Keeley had made it clear that life with her father wasn't always easy, especially now that he was slowly failing.

But spending the past few hours in their family home, enjoying a dinner and time with two people who had weathered hard times and still actually talked to each other, had tugged at Connor until he felt a raw and lonely chasm deepen in his heart.

Feelings he'd buried during what he thought would be a hopeless, lifelong incarceration were surfacing with each passing day.

What if there was still hope for new beginnings? What if Marsha had changed—and would be willing to get along, if only for their son's sake?

Putting the past behind them would make everything so much easier…

Connor pulled his cell phone from his pocket, turned it on and checked the bars as he walked out to Keeley's car. Sure enough, there was much better reception here in town than at the campground, where rocky bluffs towered over Aspen Creek and rimmed the main camping area.

He speed-dialed one of the few numbers programmed into the phone and listened to it ring, and ring, and ring… not even hopeful that there would be an answer.

"Hullo?" His ex-wife's slurred voice grated in his ear.

From the sound of her voice, she was beyond drunk, and his hope faded. He only hoped Joshua wasn't awake to see her. Then again, maybe he saw her like this so often that he thought it was normal.

"This is Connor. I wanted to tell you that—"

"I know who you are," she muttered. "A *convict*. What kid deserves a dad like you?"

He fought to keep his voice level and calm. "As I already told you, I was never guilty. It was all a mistake. I've been *exonerated*."

"Right. Only who's to say the new DNA stuff isn't wrong?"

Connor glanced at his watch. "Please, let me talk to Joshua."

"Since they gave me full custody, I'm the one making the decisions. You have no business calling him."

"Actually, I do. You may have custody, but I still have a father's rights, Marsha." He closed his eyes, feeling a chill creep down his spine as he remembered her threat to take the boy and move somewhere out on the East Coast without sharing a forwarding address. "And I also have a right to visit him."

"Just try."

"It would be better for him if we could be adults and work together. Have you told him that I've been released yet? That I want to see him?"

"I've got a new boyfriend now. A great guy, with lots of money—and Josh already thinks of him as Dad. Why mess the poor kid up?"

Her words felt like a knife twisting in his gut. Was it true or just another of her fabrications? "Josh deserves to know his real dad, Marsha—"

"Just drop it. After school's out the three of us are moving out East, and good luck finding us then."

She disconnected the call.

Connor closed his eyes and silently counted to ten. What *were* the laws on parental rights in Michigan?

From behind him, he heard Keeley clear her throat as she came down the porch steps. "Sorry it took a while. I needed to ask Dad about an idea I had, but trying to convince him of anything he doesn't think of first is like asking a mule to fly."

How much had she overheard of his phone call? "No problem."

Dusk had settled in and now the old-fashioned street lamp by the curb painted lacy patterns of light and shadow on the sidewalk. As she walked around to the driver's side of her old SUV, her blond hair gleamed like molten silver and gold, so pretty that it nearly took his breath away.

"I didn't mean to interrupt your conversation," she murmured as she buckled her seat belt and started the engine. "You seemed to be arguing with someone when I first came out on the porch, so I went back into the house for a while."

He slouched in the front seat and looked straight ahead as she shifted into Drive, debating what to say. He'd been brutally honest about his incarceration, and even about his estrangement from his family back at the ranch.

But the situation with Marsha and Josh dominated his thoughts day and night, and felt too raw, too unsettled, too painful to share. Definitely not fodder for casual conversation where he might be faced with a flood of questions he wasn't prepared to answer.

"You aren't in some kind of trouble, are you? Should I be worried about you working for me?"

"Not at all." He considered his words for a moment. "Just some...personal problems, unfortunately. Not at all relevant to the job at the store."

They drove in silence through the downtown area of

Aspen Creek and out to the campground, where she pulled to a stop by the pavilion. Several families were gathered in the shelter, playing cards at the picnic tables.

She turned sideways in her seat and rested a wrist on the steering wheel. "Maybe you could elaborate just a little. I'm now imagining street gangs and SWAT teams knocking on my door."

"None of that has ever been a part of my life." He sighed heavily. "Though they might be easier to deal with. The phone call was, unfortunately, with my ex-wife."

Keeley drew in a shaky breath, her eyes wide. "You were married—and she wants you back?"

"She would like me to disappear. Forever. But that isn't going to happen."

"You mean…you want her back?" Keeley's somber gaze searched his face. "You still love her?"

"No." He rubbed his palm over his face and exhaled slowly. "We barely tolerate each other, sad to say."

"I can't imagine how difficult that was, if neither of you was happy."

At that, he snorted. "Happy would be a rare emotion for Marsha. Especially when she's talking to me."

Keeley dropped her gaze to her hands for a long moment then slanted a look at him. "I know it's none of my business, but wouldn't it be easier to just avoid each other?"

"It isn't that simple." He looked out at the deepening dusk and the squadron of moths orbiting the nearby security light. "We stayed together for four hard years. Then she ran off with one of the guys she'd been seeing on the sly. I wouldn't have cared by then, except…" He swallowed hard. "For our son."

Keeley paled. "Y-you have a child?"

"I would've done anything to keep that marriage together, so Josh wouldn't have a broken home. Anything."

"I'm so sorry."

A familiar, heavy mantle of sorrow and regret settled over him, making it harder to breathe. "I haven't seen him in five years. I didn't want him to have memories of visiting me in prison, but maybe I was wrong."

"It must have been so hard, not seeing him grow up," Keeley murmured. "How old is he?"

"Nine. As soon as I left prison I tried to find them, but Marsha had disappeared. I started calling old friends of hers—anyone I could remember. Most refused to talk to me, but one gal finally gave me Marsha's new cell number and last known address." He swallowed hard at the memory of that conversation. "She gave it to me because she felt Josh deserved to be in better hands."

"Oh, *no*."

"I tried to get Lonnie to elaborate. All she'd say was that Marsha had lived with a string of boyfriends in recent years, still loved the party scene, and that Josh was practically raising himself. Last month Marsha took him and moved somewhere near Detroit. She has full custody, but she should have asked me—or at least should have contacted me with that new address."

"How did she end up with full...?" Keeley bit her lower lip. "Stupid question."

"She didn't even want shared custody at first. But her lawyer convinced her otherwise, in case she ever changed her mind, I guess." Connor gave a short, bitter laugh. "After I went to prison, she got full custody by default. No one thought I'd ever be released."

"So that's why you're heading for Detroit—hoping to find your son," Keeley said slowly. "I can't imagine how heart-wrenching that must be."

"I have missed him every moment of every day. Knowing he's not in a good situation makes it a thousand times worse."

"But you've talked to him, right? Sent letters?"

"I sent letters to him twice a week, the entire time I was in prison, but never heard back. I don't know if he ever got them."

"Could you call him from there?"

"With prepaid calling cards, but Marsha always refused to put him on the phone. Then she started complaining to her lawyer about 'harassment' and 'threats,' so I wasn't allowed to call them again."

Keeley sagged against her seat and shook her head. "I just don't know what to say."

"I promise you, I have never, ever, harassed anyone. Not in my entire life."

She reached across the front seat and rested her hand on his. "I believe you. Honest, I do."

He willed away the tension roiling in his stomach. "Would you let me use your laptop tomorrow?"

"You want to take it out to the campground?"

"No—just at the store, because I need the internet. Marsha says she's taking off with Josh and her new boyfriend after the last day of school. I need to know when that is."

"Of course. We can go back to town right now, if you want to."

"No need." He thought for a moment. "I also need to look up Michigan's child custody laws and try to find a lawyer. If I wait until I get there, I may run out of time."

"And in the midst of this, your truck broke down and you got stranded here. Is there someone you can call for a loan? A different car?"

"Not really. What family I have left is in Texas and, as I've mentioned, we aren't close. I've lost touch with everyone else."

"It all seems so sad," she said slowly.

"In all fairness, once I got a life sentence I made no effort to keep in touch with anyone, except Marsha and Josh. What was the point?"

"Maybe you could go to a bank and…"

He held back a bitter laugh. "Yes, indeed, with my current employment record, my valuable collateral and my most recent address in Montana, I'm sure I sound like a *good* risk to a banker."

She gave his hand a squeeze, her lovely face etched with regret and other emotions he couldn't read in the darkness. "I wish I could help, honest. But things here are a bit shaky for me right now. I've been having trouble just trying to stay afloat."

"I couldn't ask you for money anyway. I don't want to drag anyone else into this mess."

"I'm just so *sorry* to hear about what you've been going through."

"I'm grateful for the temporary job. Working any hours I can get will help with truck repairs and give me more to work with when I get to Detroit." He opened the passenger-side door to step out into the unseasonably sultry night, then turned back to her. "If I can find a reasonable lawyer, every last penny for legal fees is going to matter when I try to get my son back."

"Your son is a very lucky boy to have a father like you." She turned the key in the ignition and then met his gaze once more. "And I promise, I'll be keeping you both in my prayers."

Long after she drove away, Connor stared after her.

If not for this entire, difficult situation, they never would have met. But what would his life be like now if he'd known someone like her years ago?

Gentle and thoughtful, with a caring heart, Keeley

wouldn't have fallen for a bronc rider from Texas back then, any more than she would now. He was hardly the right fit for her world. He had to leave, to go after his son and then find a job in the world he knew best—cattle ranching or horses out West.

And he knew she couldn't leave.

Her roots went deep in this pretty little town—her father was failing, and the business she was trying to save would keep her here, while there was no way he could stay. Even if he got custody of his son and wanted to come back, he'd be as well suited to a tourist town as a bull in a ballet.

But he would help Keeley as best he could before leaving Aspen Creek, and build some memories to savor after he was gone, because he already knew he would never forget her.

And those memories would have to be enough.

Chapter Seven

Keeley stepped out of the Aspen Creek Community Church and shaded her eyes against the bright morning sun.

"How are you all?" she said, grinning to the slender, auburn-haired woman and her son, who were waiting at the bottom of the steps.

Sophie Alexander-McLaren rested a hand on her son Eli's shoulder and nodded toward her new husband, who was talking to another parishioner. "Doing well. He's busier than ever at his clinic and hopes to hire another doctor this fall. I'm still working just three days a week, but that's all we want, really. I'm needed at home, too."

"We've missed you at the book club," Keeley teased. "Monday mornings aren't the same without you."

Sophie whispered something to her son and he ran to join his father. "We've just finished six weeks with a new therapist," she said in a lowered voice. "She gave us all some great ideas for working with him and encouraged us to sign him up for a new autism spectrum disorder program through the university."

"I'm so glad. He's such a sweet boy."

"He's still obsessed with motorcycles and dinosaurs, of course, but she also introduced us to some new programs for his iPad." She laughed. "He thinks they're games, but they're supposed to help him a lot."

Keeley gave her a quick hug. "Wonderful news, all around."

"That it is." Sophie cocked an eyebrow. "And what's this I hear about you?"

Keeley felt a faint blush warm her cheeks. "Nothing much—except for Edna retiring Thursday. I miss her already."

"Ah, but I hear there's someone new in your life—a tall, dark and yummy cowboy from out West?" Sophie winked at her. "He ought to be luring lots of the local ladies into the store."

"That wasn't the plan," Keeley said dryly. "He was on his way east and his truck bit the dust. He'll only be in town for three weeks at the most—maybe less. He's just putting in some hours at the store while he waits for repairs."

Sophie chuckled. "That isn't how I heard it down at the coffee shop this morning. Lucy was telling everyone how this good-looking cowboy came to your rescue like some medieval knight when you were stranded on the roof of your store. Very romantic, according to her. Well, except the part about your dad. Oops."

Keeley groaned. "Lucy wasn't even there. It was Millie from the knitting shop. But between the two of them, I wouldn't be surprised to see the story hit *USA TODAY*—though why anyone would care is beyond me."

"They all sure do at the coffee shop when Lucy starts spinning her tales. She's quite the storyteller."

"So…she said something about my dad?"

"Something about him 'driving like a crazy old coot and knocking down your ladder…and it's a wonder you weren't killed.'" Sophie bit her lower lip. "I suppose he isn't going to be too happy when he learns about the gossip."

"*Livid* would just about sum it up. And he'll probably imagine the incident *and* the gossip was my fault."

"I'm so sorry, sweetie. I know it isn't easy watching over him these days. Any luck talking him into health-care aide visits? Or a housekeeper who could also watch over him?"

Keeley rolled her eyes. "The last time I brought that up he nearly threw me out of his house. Even finding a renter or two for the little cottages out back could add some subtle supervision, but he isn't interested in that, either. Nope, it's still just me—and that's only when he's in a good mood."

"You do know that my husband will write medical recommendations and do whatever he can to help you get your dad into a facility when the time comes. Not," Sophie added quickly, "that Paul's at that point yet. But still..."

"Good Lord willing, it will be a long time off, because he will fight that idea until he's absolutely unable to care for himself. He knows his legal rights and isn't about to give up."

Sophie's husband beckoned to her and she waved back, then gave Keeley another hug. "I promise I'll try to make it to Beth's Bookstore tomorrow for coffee with you all. But if you ever need help of any kind, just let me know."

Keeley watched Sophie and her family walk toward the parking lot and sighed. Sophie was an excellent physical therapist, but no one really knew just how challenging Paul North could be—or how stubborn.

Despite the bright sunshine and perfect, seventy-degree weather, business was slow for a Sunday afternoon. Keeley drove out to the hardware store for supplies then asked Connor to replace the wobbly, dripping faucet in the customer bathroom and install new dead bolts on the front and back doors.

While he was working on that, she settled at the front counter with a cup of hot strawberry tea and hit the speed-dial number for her sister.

Liza answered on the second ring, sounding harried. From the commotion in the background, apparently neither toddler was taking an afternoon nap.

"Is this a bad time? Should I call back later?"

Liza groaned. "Wouldn't make much difference. The twins were up early this morning, show no signs of slowing down, and the one who desperately needs a nap is me."

"Maybe Owen can take over for a while so you can."

"Great idea—but he's already on his way to Boston for a meeting tomorrow morning."

"Bad timing."

Liza laughed. "Your time will come, Keel. Did you know adults can survive on almost no sleep for days?"

Keeley shuddered. "Really?"

"Nope. You are talking to a complete zom— Annie, put that *down*. You cannot hit your sister!"

Keeley heard the sound of footsteps then the squeal of a freezer door being pulled open. "Um, everything all right?"

"I just gave the wild bunch orange Popsicles. That ought to keep them busy for two minutes. By the way, I got a phone call from your old boyfriend Todd yesterday. I'm sure our brother got a call, too."

Keeley's heart sank. "He was never a boyfriend and you know it. He had absolutely no business calling you."

"That's what I thought. Still, I've been meaning to email you. What's this about some murderer working in your store? That just can't be true." There was a long pause. "Can it?"

"Connor was exonerated—I hope Todd told you that. But, well…he is the reason I'm calling you."

Liza gasped. "Keeley!"

"He's a really nice guy and he needs your help." She quickly explained Connor's background and why she'd hired him. "The thing is, he'll soon be on his way to Michigan to see his son, and he's worried about the boy's welfare. He's hoping to regain at least partial custody."

"That won't be easy." Liza fell silent for a moment. "You do know I'm a tax attorney, not an expert in family law."

"Of course I do. But would you have any advice for him? I know he's really short of money right now, after being incarcerated for so long. I don't know how much legal representation he can afford."

"Honestly, I'm swamped right now and he needs a different kind of lawyer. I don't know what help I can give him."

"Please—can you do a little research? Or talk to someone who would know? I'll…" Keeley took a deep breath. "I'll come up to Minneapolis and help you with the twins for a whole weekend."

"Whoa. *Really?*"

"Promise. It has to be around the end of August, though. There's a bit of a lull in tourism then, before the fall and holiday seasons start."

"Deal. Have him call me this afternoon sometime after three, okay? With a lot of prayer, the girls might be sleeping then. And, Keel? You really do think you're doing the right thing, having this guy working at the store? Do you honestly trust him?"

"I saw the newspaper clipping about his release. Better than that, Lorraine at the sheriff's office verified his story." Keeley smiled to herself, imagining her younger sister in warrior mode, ready to protect anyone in the family at a moment's notice. "And, yes, I think he's a good man. And I like him. A lot."

Liz fell silent for a moment. "Oh, sweetie. You *like* him. As in, getting involved?"

"Honestly, I wish I could. But don't worry. He's only focused on his son and how soon he can fight for custody—and after that, I think he'll be heading for Texas or Montana. End of story." Keeley gave a short, deprecating laugh. "Anyway, you know my track record. Relationships never last and I've almost given up. They just aren't worth the heartbreak."

The bells over the front door of the shop jangled and Millie Ferguson held the front door open as she peered warily into the store. She stepped inside when she saw Keeley at the front counter.

Keeley set aside the stack of invoices in front of her and smiled. "How are you today, Millie?"

Millie craned her wattled neck, searching out the corners of the store before coming all the way in. "Is that… that cowboy working here?"

Keeley rolled her eyes. "As of yesterday morning, yes. He'll be here for just a few weeks. Can I help you?"

Millie leaned across the counter and lowered her voice. "Do you think that's a good idea, dear? I mean, what do you know about a stranger like that?"

"Enough. Is there something worrying you?"

"Well, I…I…" She lifted her chin, determination glinting in her faded blue eyes. "I was down at the coffee shop this morning, and Deputy Hansmann was there having breakfast. I overheard him telling another deputy that this new employee of yours is a troublemaker. I just wanted to make sure you knew about it. You can't trust anyone these days. Especially some stranger who just waltzes into town all sneaky-like, ready to take advantage of some gullib—uh...innocent woman."

A sneaky *waltzer*? The words conjured up a strange image and Keeley bit back a laugh. The woman could say more without taking a breath than anyone she'd ever met, but she didn't always make sense.

"I checked out Connor thoroughly and I believe he's a good, honest man. There may be a little gossip in town, but I'm just thankful that you'd never be a part of that, right?"

Flustered now, the older woman bobbed her head and backed away from the counter. "Oh, no. Of course not."

Keeley nodded her approval. "I'm so glad people like you still have class. So, are you all set for the Antique Walk next weekend?"

"Um...yes. I hope so."

"I'm sure you'll draw a lot of business. You've done a wonderful job with your window display—very colorful." Keeley smiled. "Looking at all of those beautiful yarns makes me wish I knew how to knit."

"Thank you." Millie darted another uneasy glance around the shop, her brow furrowed, as if expecting to see Hannibal Lecter ready to pounce. "I— Well, I'd better be on my way."

Millie hurried out the door and crossed Main diagonally toward her own store. Keeley watched her unlock the front door and slip inside, then turned to fetch more millefiori paperweights from the storeroom for her own front window display.

She nearly ran into Connor, who stood in the storeroom doorway with a tool belt slung across his hips and a Schlage lock-set box in his hands.

"I've got the back door done," he said quietly.

"I suppose you overheard our local busybody," Keeley said with a sigh. "I'm really sorry about that."

"It's no more than I expected. I'm just surprised she didn't mention the ex-con part."

"Actually, I'm surprised, too. But maybe she didn't quite dare. She seemed edgy, probably thinking you were going to appear. Deputy Todd sure didn't hesitate to share that detail with my sister, Liza—who's clear off in Minneapolis. The stinker."

"He called your *sister*?"

"We all grew up together, same schools since kindergarten. He had a crush on her in third grade, and I suppose he still thinks he'll get brownie points from her if he tattles." Keeley snorted. "A sad commentary on him, to say the least. He's like Aspen Creek's version of Barney Fife."

Connor shook his head as he headed for the front door. "I don't care who knows the truth. I just don't want it to hurt you or your business. For the short amount of time I'll be here, there's no way I want to cause collateral damage."

She knew he meant it and his concern warmed her heart. "When you get the front lock done, take the rest of the afternoon to use my laptop and the internet."

He gave her a startled glance. "I should do it after work. You sure aren't paying me to sit at a desk."

She waved a hand dismissively. "Start now. The more prepared you are, the better chance you have. It might take a lot longer than you think just wading through Michigan's custody laws. And be sure to print off anything you need."

He hesitated for a long moment then finally nodded. "Okay, but I'll pay you back."

"No need. Oh—and be sure to call Liza at three sharp."

He looked up from unscrewing the old dead bolt and gave her a blank look. "Your sister?"

"She's an attorney. Not in family law, and she's not in the right state, but maybe she can give you some advice."

He sighed heavily. "I know I need all the advice I can

get, but I just don't have the extra money. I'll have to pay for a lawyer in Michigan."

"You don't need to pay Liza a cent. She's doing this for me...and believe me, she's actually grateful for the opportunity."

"I...I just can't take advantage of her like that. Or you," he added wearily. "You've already done too much."

Keeley laughed. "I'm watching her little hooligans for a weekend in exchange for this, so don't worry about taking *plenty* of time on the phone. Hours. If I survive that weekend, she'll still owe me no matter how long you two talk."

Chapter Eight

Connor had left prison with a bitter heart over the years he'd lost and the God who had forsaken him. With grim awareness, he'd accepted that his life would never be the same.

So when he'd arrived in Aspen Creek with a nearly empty wallet and dimming hopes of reaching Detroit in time to find his son, he'd expected to be met with frank suspicion, not trust and acceptance.

He'd never expected that anyone in an upscale vacation area like this one would consider hiring him—much less a pretty young woman who trusted him with her store, her clientele and her cash register...and who seemed determined to help him in whatever way she could.

Though whether he'd encountered someone like her by chance or something more divine, he couldn't guess. After so many years of silence in response to his prayers, he had fallen away. So why would God start caring about him now?

Connor pushed away from the desk in the corner of the back room and sorted through the stack of papers he'd printed from numerous Montana and Michigan legal websites. He stapled them into sets and tapped the pages into a neat pile.

The time on the internet had been invaluable and nothing he could have taken care of out at the park. That Keeley had trusted him with her computer was yet another favor that he was thankful for. How could he ever repay her for all she'd done?

"Can I interrupt?" Keeley appeared at the doorway with a mug of coffee and a plate of frosted sugar cookies. "You probably need a boost after wading through all of that information."

He eyed the pastel cookies and inhaled the light, lemony scent. "I feel guilty spending this time for my own purposes and being plied with food, to boot. You'll be taking these hours off my paycheck, I hope."

She waved away his concern. "Not an issue. You were here, and that let me run over to check on Dad twice without needing to lock up. That's value enough for me. Did you discover anything good?"

"I wasn't sure if Marsha had a right to take Joshua from Montana to Michigan without notifying me. There have been varied legal opinions on this, but apparently, as the sole custodial parent, she did have that right. Especially if she were to claim that the move was in his best interests."

"And do you think it was?"

He shrugged. "She—or her lawyer—could claim that her move to a more urban setting in Detroit meant better schools than a small town in Montana, and closer proximity to good medical and dental care. That wasn't her intent, because I hear she was really just following a new boyfriend, but a lawyer could give it a good spin."

"What about your visitation rights? Can she prevent you from seeing him?"

"She has both legal and physical custody, which I didn't

contest when I thought I'd be locked away for life. I want to pursue shared custody again. But no matter what, I still have a right to see Josh—unless a court terminates my parental rights altogether."

"She wouldn't try to have that done, would she?"

"I doubt she has the money, but I wouldn't put it past her to try." He took a long swallow of coffee. "That would involve proving abuse, which she could never prove. Or having me deemed unfit—and prison time might cover that one."

"Oh, Connor. That's awful. Even though you were exonerated?"

"It shouldn't, but that's a question I'll have for your sister." He glanced at the clock on the wall. "Guess I'd better make that call."

"Use the desk phone so you won't use up your cell minutes. Liza is number three on the speed-dial keypad. While you two talk, I'm going back up front to work on my window display."

Connor rubbed the back of his neck as he studied the list of questions he'd compiled for Keeley's sister. Doubt gnawed at his stomach.

Marsha could be kind and loving on a good day, but she could also be manipulative and difficult, and had often complained about the constraints of parenthood. Would she fight him on this?

Given her attitude during their last phone conversation, that answer was a definite yes—but whether it was out of spite, revenge or true love for Joshua, he couldn't say.

Liza answered on the second ring. "So, this is Keeley's cowboy? I see from the caller ID you're at the store."

"Right."

"You do know that I'm a tax lawyer and not in family

law, correct? I can only provide my opinion, but you need the right kind of counsel when you actually do proceed."

"Understood."

"And since your ex is in Michigan, you should have an attorney who works there. Laws vary from state to state, as do the interpretations of those laws…and all that can shift in a given year. So you need someone who is sharp and who keeps up to date."

"Figured that, too."

She gave a short, humorless laugh. "From what I've heard plus that Texas accent, you must be one of those laconic loner types. Tell me, cowboy, is my sister safe with you there? Did you tell her the whole truth about your past?"

"Yes, ma'am. And she checked it out at the sheriff's office. Someone named Lorraine looked it all up."

"Lorraine, okay. If you'd told me Todd did the research, I'd have my doubts. So, fire away. What do you want to know?"

"What are the chances that I can get custody?"

"I just talked to a friend who practices family law here in Minneapolis and gave her the basics. First of all—even though you were exonerated—five years in prison is still a strike against you."

"I was afraid of that."

"Second, the boy has been with his mother for five years, so the courts would hesitate to take him away from her. Unless there's documented abuse or neglect, your chances for full custody are slim."

"Partial custody?"

"You'd have a better chance of that."

Liza fell silent for a moment. "If you do get shared custody, record every time she doesn't show up or is late…and any negative statements she makes. If she's lackadaisical, maybe you can get full custody. And if she's wrapped up in her social life, she might even be glad to give it to you."

Connor looked down at his list of questions. "Would a mediator help?"

"Just a minute—my house phone is ringing. I'm going to put you on hold."

Connor leaned back in his chair and surveyed the cluttered bulletin board above the desk. Invoices. Cryptic reminders on colorful Post-it notes. To-do lists.

But the photos—those were the best part. He leaned closer to study them. There were several dozen, at least. Grade-school photos of four kids spanning several years. With front teeth. Without. Shy smiles, goofy smiles. Keeley's nieces and nephews?

And then there were the family photos of various family groups by a tree at Christmas. Easter, with the little ones proudly holding colorful baskets. Summer photos at a lake. Keeley had to be the family photographer, because she was in so few of them, but there was one that caught his eye and he gently lifted off the thumbtack to see it better.

Keeley, her blond hair gleaming in the bright sun, with her father and another man and woman beside her—her siblings, maybe—surrounded by kids and dogs.

All of them seemed so happy, so relaxed, that his breath caught.

Once again he wondered what his life would have been like if he'd found someone like Keeley, with a good heart and a kind soul, instead of falling for a buckle bunny with tight jeans and an "I'm yours if you want me" glance.

He'd been lonely then, on the road month after month following the rodeo circuit, and in Marsha's bold gaze he'd imagined a connection, a relationship far deeper than just an evening in a raucous honky-tonk bar.

She was one of the many mistakes he'd made—except

that she'd given him a beautiful son, and that he could never regret.

Liza came back on the line. "Sorry about that. From what I found on the internet, I think a mediator in Michigan only deals with existing custody arrangements—scheduling problems and such. But you'd better double-check to make sure."

"Do you think there's any chance of finding pro bono services that could help with this?"

"I doubt it. A custody battle can be long, hard and costly, and an attorney's time alone can easily reach ten or twelve grand."

Connor sat back in his chair, speechless.

"You might find an attorney who will let you make payments, though," she added gently. "I'm sure most parents struggle with these costs. Good luck, and God bless."

Long after she disconnected, Connor stared at the family images on the wall, his heart aching for the photos he longed to have with Joshua at his side. Confirmation. High-school graduation. Vacations and adventures and Christmas mornings.

But ten or twelve *grand*?

The amount was so far beyond his reach that it might as well be a million. Yet there was no way that he was going to give up. His son deserved a better life, with a father who loved him with all his heart.

And whatever it took, Connor was going to make it happen.

Chapter Nine

Stepping into the warm glow of Beth's Bookstore early on Monday mornings, with its soft classical music and wonderful scents of books, bakery goods and coffee, invariably made Keeley feel deeply content. Today, with fog and light drizzle, the cozy atmosphere inside was as comforting as a warm hug.

She hoped she felt as good when she finished this morning's mission.

Though the book-club members continually evolved as old friends moved away and new members were drawn by the poster in the front window, most of the mainstays still came. This morning, however, only Beth, Sophie and Olivia were seated at the back meeting area with cups of steaming coffee cradled in their hands.

The three looked as bright and cheery as a trio of colorful songbirds, with Beth in a long paisley skirt and orange T-shirt, Sophie in her lime clinic uniform splashed with cherries, and Olivia in an elegant violet pantsuit that flattered her closely cropped silver hair.

"Good morning." Keeley smiled at them as she made her way to the Keurig on a side table and prepared a cup of the blueberry-flavored coffee generously lightened with a splash of skim, then selected a lemon poppy-seed muffin from an overflowing tray of treats. "Are you all ready for what this week will bring?"

Tucking a wayward strand of chestnut hair back into the casual twist at her nape, Beth nodded. "We're planning to have a sidewalk sale during the festival and some local authors will be doing readings inside the store each day. My mother will be helping with cookie decorating back in the children's area—Dr. Seuss–shaped cutouts."

"Eli will love that," Sophie exclaimed. "If she needs help supervising, I'd be happy to pitch in on Saturday."

"That sounds more fun than my job," Olivia grumbled as she nibbled the edge of a cranberry-and-white-chocolate scone. "I'll be the cashier at the church food tent for eight hours straight on Friday."

"My plans aren't quite what they were when I still had Edna." Keeley clasped her coffee mug between her hands, savoring the warmth. "We were quite a team."

Olivia lifted a perfectly arched eyebrow. "I hear you have some new help, though. Quite an interesting fellow—or so they say."

Keeley stilled. "Oh?"

"I needed more of that nice thick yarn for making prayer shawls, so I stopped by Knitting Pretty and, of course, I also got an ample dose of local news." Olivia smirked. "Not that I wanted to hear it, but it can be a bit hard getting away, as you know."

"I can guess what she wanted to share," Keeley said dryly.

Olivia and Beth exchanged a quick, concerned glance. Then Olivia cleared her throat. "Word has apparently traveled rather fast about that cowboy of yours. Are you sure it's a good idea to have him working in your store?"

Sophie's confused gaze swept all of them. "So what's

wrong with him? I thought he sounded like quite a hero, rescuing Keeley from her roof like that."

Keeley bit back a sigh. Small-town life was wonderful, and she'd never wanted to live anywhere else. But while close relationships and a deep sense of community were great, the tendency for persistent gossip was not.

"I think they're referring to his incarceration," she said, meeting Olivia's gaze. "Would that sum it up?"

The older woman didn't flinch. "I would say so, yes."

Keeley gave her a level glance. "Honestly, I think he turned up in answer to my prayer."

Olivia shook her head. "Some people in town think you're making a foolish mistake."

"Most people should know Millie is an unreliable gossip, and Todd is, as well, even though he has seen proof and knows Connor was innocent of any crime. So if he's dramatizing the story down at the coffee shop, then he and I need to have another talk."

"So have you seen that proof yourself?" Sophie whispered.

"Yes, I have." Keeley resisted the urge to throw up her hands in frustration. "I think he's a good man, caught in terrible circumstances, who is trying to make a new life for himself. Can you guess what his one goal is now? What he wants more than anything?"

Beth shrugged. "Vengeance, maybe. Or a ton of money for selling his story to a magazine?"

"A deal with a major book publisher and a ghost writer?" Olivia offered.

"Not even close." Keeley felt her lower lip tremble and she took a steadying breath. "All he wants is to find his nine-year-old son, do everything he can to regain at least partial custody, then find a good, steady job somewhere.

He's not thinking fame or fortune or book deals. He simply wants to be a good father to his boy."

Sophie leaned back in her chair and fanned herself. "Oh, my. Tall, dark and *awesome*. Be still, my heart."

"He won't be here long—only a few weeks, until his truck is done. So if you overhear anything, please—just tell people the truth."

Connor had firmly declined Keeley's offer of a ride to work this morning, so with an hour until opening her store, she drove slowly away from the bookstore, cruised past the sheriff's office and then drove through town searching for Todd's patrol car.

He should be out on the highway trapping speeders or somewhere out in the county on a call, but his mornings were usually spent in town at his favorite haunt.

She found him at the coffee shop, as she'd expected—hunched over his morning coffee and a massive cinnamon roll slathered with caramel and pecans—chatting with the waitress.

She settled on the stool next to him and ordered a cup of coffee. The waitress, a heavyset, middle-aged woman with Dora on her name tag, brought it in a flash then disappeared into the kitchen.

"Mornin', Keel." Todd shot a sideways glance at her then studied his coffee mug.

"I suppose you can guess why I'm here." She glanced around, but the shop was nearly empty save for an older couple in a booth at the far corner. She lowered her voice. "I've been running into an interesting situation and thought you'd want to know."

He took a slow swallow of his coffee.

"Millie stopped by and was worried about the 'troublemaker' working for me. Several of my friends are concerned about the 'murderer' in town. Even my sister heard about it, and *she* lives in Minneapolis." She glared at Todd's profile until he finally turned to meet her eyes. "This has got to stop. You know the truth about Connor, yet this so-called news is spreading like wildfire and I know you're partly to blame. How fair is that?"

"I admit I discussed it privately here—in a back booth, with the deputy who works the eastern half of the county." He shrugged, blowing off her concern. "If someone overheard, well…"

"Like Millie, of all people? Or a *waitress*?"

His gaze slid away.

"And what about my sister?"

Crimson splotches bloomed on his plump cheeks. "I was just concerned about having someone like him around."

"No, you like to entertain people with your dramatic stories." Keeley gritted her teeth. "And calling Liz was so over the top that I should report you to the sheriff. You had no business doing that. I'm thirty-one and make decisions on my own. I can hire circus clowns to run my store if I want to."

As a kid he'd been a tattletale and a gossip, and had bullied younger kids. How he'd managed to snag a fiancée was hard to believe. How he'd become a deputy was beyond her comprehension.

"I know. It's just…it's just that I see things you'd never want to see, Keel. Controlling, conniving, dangerous guys. Girlfriends or wives too terrified to even try to get away. So when someone shows up with a troubled past, well…"

"That has nothing to do with Connor. He's a nice guy who suffered an unjust conviction, and anyway, he's just a very temporary employee."

"Guilty or not, he's been rubbing shoulders with convicts for five years—probably nurturing a lot of hate and resentment over his conviction." Todd ran his fingers through his thinning hair. "What did that do to him, huh? Not affect him at all?"

"You're saying that people don't have a choice—that even a good person would turn bad in prison, despite their nature? Their upbringing? I don't believe that."

He fidgeted with a menu. "I'd dealt with a case of fraud perpetrated on an elderly widow with dementia just before your new buddy showed up in town, and it made me think."

"He isn't my 'new buddy,' and you can't imagine that I'm like that poor old woman." She sighed. Todd apparently thought he was doing the right thing, and she knew it was nearly impossible to change his mind. "I trust you won't be sharing details about him with everyone else in town. Right?"

"Promise." He cleared his throat. "Unless there's a good reason."

She dug through her purse and tucked a five under her coffee mug. "I just wish the gossip mill around here wasn't so ready to brand Connor as something he's not. And, anyway, he'll be on the road for Detroit the very day his truck is fixed. We'll never see him again, I'm sure."

"We can only hope," Todd muttered as she stood to leave. "But in the meantime, you'd better be careful."

Stifling a sharp retort, she lifted a shoulder in a noncommittal shrug and headed outside, frustration and anger tying her stomach into a heavy knot.

She'd spoken offhandedly about Connor's departure, as if it didn't matter to her.

But it did. Way too much.

With every passing day she found herself falling for him a little bit more as she experienced his deep sense of honor, his warmth and kindness, and an indefinable, physical attraction that made her nerves tingle and her knees weaken if their eyes happened to meet.

But she'd always known he needed to leave, fight for his son and then establish a new life. His goals had been clear from the very start. Her roots—her business, her debts, her failing father—made it impossible to ever follow.

And once again she'd be facing inevitable heartbreak. When would she ever learn?

Chapter Ten

By Tuesday business had started to pick up. There were browsers in the store all day long and, with his third day of work, Connor had begun to slip into a comfortable routine—something he'd never expected could happen the day he'd accepted the job.

He worked on maintenance projects around the place unless Keeley needed to go check on her dad—then he manned the cash register and tried to revive his rusty social skills with the customers who stopped by.

More than a few, he suspected, were locals curious about Keeley's new employee—like the two teenage girls who were now giggling together over by an antique jewelry display.

They whispered, their heads together, but now and then one of them shot a look in his direction. Belatedly, he realized that they could be surreptitiously shoplifting, so he strolled over and leaned a hip against the display case.

"Howdy, ladies. Finding anything you like?"

The brunette blushed deep pink and ducked her head. The one with long blond hair pulled up in a high ponytail blushed, too, but she lifted her chin and brazened it out. "We're just looking around for a birthday gift."

"Your mom? Or a friend?"

They exchanged glances. "Friend," blurted the brunette. "Um, a girlfriend. At school."

Well…that was certainly awkward, and reeked of guilt. Still, he hadn't seen them pocket anything and the display on top of the locked glass case appeared intact.

The bells over the front door tinkled and Bobby Whidbey walked in, bent beneath the weight of his school backpack. His face lit up with a broad smile when he spied Connor. "Hello, Mr. Rafferty. I'm here! Hi, Sara. Hi, Elise!"

The girls looked at each other and snickered, then sidled past Connor and zoomed toward the front door.

Bobby watched them leave, his expression filled with innocent adoration, oblivious to their arrogant slight.

Connor felt his heart turn over. Things hadn't changed since he'd been in high school himself, which was a sad commentary on just how heartless teenagers could be.

"Those are nice girls," Bobby said. "And really pretty, too. I see them at school sometimes."

"Are they nice to you? Do they talk to you at school?"

He thought for a moment, his brow furrowed as he processed his answer. "They're busy," he said finally, with a single, decisive nod. "They dance at football games and everything."

"Cheerleaders?"

"Yeah."

From their snide response to Bobby as they left, Connor guessed they were in the most popular clique at school, were full of themselves and in fact weren't kind to him at all.

"Keeley left us both our orders for while she takes her dad to the doctor's office," Connor said. "Are you ready to work?"

"I'm the sweeping boss." Bobby's voice rang with pride.

"Exactly right. And you're very good at it, too. I watched you working yesterday and I was impressed." Connor reached for a sheet of paper on the front counter. "She says here that you get to sweep the floors, collect the trash and take it to the Dumpster out back. You also get to feed and water Rags. We'll leave it at just that for now."

Bobby dropped his backpack behind the counter and hurried to the back room, where the sound of industrious sweeping soon filled the air, punctuated by occasional sneezes.

A few minutes later a middle-aged man scurried in, checked his watch and then made a beeline for Connor. His narrow face, undershot jaw and twitchy motions reminded Connor of a rabbit.

"I need a gift for my wife and I need it fast. Any ideas? I have no clue. I'm meeting her for an early dinner in about an hour, and I forgot our anniversary." He scowled. "I will hear about it for months if she finds out."

The challenge of "the blind leading the blind" came to mind, but Connor summoned up a smile and tried to remember how Keeley handled her more befuddled male customers.

"Would she like something personal? There's antique jewelry over in the case, and scarves are on the rack in the corner. Women seem to like both, far as I can tell." Connor gestured to the back of the store. "Or would she like something for the house?"

The man's panicked gaze darted around the room then landed on a giant antique basket filled with dried flowers, plus what appeared to be weeds and cattails. "That thing—over there."

Really? "Uh...great choice."

"Wrap it in a nice big box, some sort of shiny paper and a big bow. Extra-big bow. I want it to look elegant." The guy checked his watch again. "And make it snappy. Like I said, I'm in a hurry."

Make it *snappy*? The man was a good foot shorter than Connor, but he'd still managed to look down his nose while giving orders.

With a sigh, Connor eyed the bulky arrangement. "We don't have gift boxes that big. But with that one, it's sort of like giving fresh flowers—and those you wouldn't wrap."

"A fancy gift bag, then?" The man drummed his fingernails on the counter. "Surely you have those."

"Yes, but probably not that large. Let me check." Connor leaned down to check the supply shelves below the cash register and shook his head. "Afraid not. But I could put a bow on the side of the basket…or you could pick something else."

"Really? That's the best you can do?" He snarled. A red flush started climbing up his pale face and now the veins at his temples stood out in sharp relief. "Where is Keeley?"

"Errands. But she'll be back within the hour. If you want to come back then—"

"I *told* you I was in a hurry, and *this* was a total waste of my time." He spun around, jerked the front door open and left, slamming it so hard that a glassware display in the front window rattled.

Temper, temper, Connor thought, shaking his head. Since Keeley left there'd been three pleasant customers and one complete jerk.

He headed to the back room, where he'd been re-caulking the windows between customers. "Hey, Bobby, would you like a Coke? My treat."

The storeroom was silent, the broom lying on the floor by the back door.

"Bobby?" He scanned the area, glanced at the employee

restroom. The lights were off, the door partly open. "Are you back here?"

Nothing stirred.

He glanced around once more then checked the front of the store. Maybe the kid had gone home for some reason?

It wasn't until he went to the back again that he heard the softest rustle of movement and a faint whimper. "Bobby? Are you all right?"

He found the boy curled up in a tight ball, cowering behind a stack of boxes in the corner. "Bobby. It's me, Connor. What's wrong?"

If anything, the boy tried to melt even further against the wall, his arms wrapped tightly around his knees and his face hidden.

Baffled, Connor hunkered down close to him and nearly rested a comforting hand on his back, then hesitated. "What happened? Are you hurt?"

Silence…then a soft whimper and a nearly imperceptible shake of his head.

"I was sure hoping you wanted to take a little break. There's some soda in the fridge and Keeley left us some of those pretty purple cookies."

Those offerings would have easily won him over when Connor was that age, but the boy didn't budge. A silent sob shook through him, though, and at that Connor lowered himself to the floor, stretched out his legs and leaned against a shelf, close enough for support without actual contact.

Lonnie's recent words about his ex-wife flashed into his thoughts. *Joshua is practically raising himself.*

He had no doubt about the truth of Lonnie's statement, and even now it tore at his heart. Who was there for his son, when he was sad or lonely or scared, if Marsha was off partying with her friends? Did she ever bother to get a babysitter or was he left alone? Did he feel as helpless as this poor boy next to him?

"I've been having quite a day," Connor murmured. "How about you? Let's see… This morning, I woke up to find a raccoon rummaging through my campsite. It broke into my cooler and made off with my hot dogs, buns and apples. And last night my tent leaked. Lucky we had just a gentle rain."

Bobby didn't move or say anything, but he emanated the terror of a trapped animal and Connor felt utterly helpless. He'd known from their first hello yesterday that this was a special-needs child, but what on earth had happened to him just now?

"So after the store closes, I need to stop at the hardware store for tent patching material and at the grocery store to replace what that raccoon stole," Connor continued. He kept his voice soft and low, as he always had when halter-breaking a foal or stepping aboard a green two-year-old for the first time, and just kept up a continual stream of quiet words. "Have you ever had a run-in with a raccoon? That was a first for me. I think—"

A key turned in the back door lock and Keeley breezed inside with a couple of grocery sacks in her hand. She gave Connor a startled look. Then her gaze veered to Bobby and her face filled with compassion. "Oh, my."

"He's upset, and I don't know why. He's been like this for maybe twenty minutes."

The bells over the front door tinkled.

Ignoring the arrival of customers, she dropped her purse and groceries on the worktable and knelt on the floor. She rested her hand on Connor's shoulder. "I'll take care of this, if you can just watch the front of the store. I'll talk to you about this later."

* * *

After talking to Bobby for twenty minutes, Keeley fortified him with a cheeseburger and malt at the coffee shop down the street, then took him home to the dreary clapboard house out behind the Pine Cone Tap at the edge of town.

Just six blocks from Main, it was like another world back there—a hardscrabble tumble of shabby homes and the hulking wrecks of abandoned cars jacked up on blocks. Despite the efforts of the mayor and town council, it devolved back down into hardship acres as fast as anyone tried to clean it up.

No one was home, as usual, or she would have had yet another private talk with his aunt Bess. With a sigh, she watched Bobby walk into the unlocked house, dragging his backpack.

She would try again tomorrow.

Back at the store by five, she found Connor ringing up a sale for the mayor's wife and busied herself in the storeroom until the woman left to avoid a lengthy bout of chatter.

"I talked to Bobby for twenty minutes. Then I bought him a cheeseburger and a Coke and took him home," she said on a long sigh as she joined Connor at the cash register. "But I wish there was more I could do."

Connor's eyes were wary. "I have no idea what happened. One minute he was happy. The next he was cringing in that corner."

"It was nothing to do with you, believe me. And, honestly, I hardly know where to begin." She paced the floor, thinking about what she'd seen and heard about Bobby's sad life. And once again, she felt tears burn beneath her eyelids. "Bobby was born normal, as far as anyone knows. But his father was an abuser who beat his wife to death one night and didn't stop with her—he laid into Bobby and nearly killed him, too. A four-year-old child. Can you believe it? I hope that man never, ever, gets out of prison.

"Bobby suffered brain damage and multiple fractures. That's why he walks a little funny, and why his mental abilities are slow." She drew in a long, steadying breath. "I know other kids are mean to him because he's different, but if I overhear it, those kids get a talking-to they won't soon forget. I even call their parents and report it to the principal at school for whatever good that could do, and I tell those kids exactly what I'm going to do. But it still happens—and it breaks my heart. After all he went through, he doesn't deserve any more pain."

At the ravaged look in Connor's eyes, she wondered if he was thinking about his own son, whose wayward mother might have lived with just such a man without regard for the boy's safety.

"Who takes care of Bobby now?"

"His aunt. I think she does care for him, but she's uneducated, obese, and has trouble walking, so he doesn't have many opportunities. Even with welfare, she works part-time in a seedy bar to make ends meet. So now and then I take him out and buy him some decent clothes. Otherwise the kids would just tease him more."

"And you gave him a job."

"So he'll have money for school supplies and whatever it is that kids want at that age. He's such a sweet boy."

Connor shook his head slowly, his expression grim. "Can't the county step in? The social workers?"

"I don't know all the details. I've tried to find out through the county and at school, but I'm not family and privacy rights prevail these days. For all I know, he might have gotten counseling in the past, but if that's true, he needs more of it."

"So he's basically falling between the cracks."

Keeley nodded. "And it breaks my heart. I've learned that if a child is fed, healthy, gets to school every day and doesn't show physical signs of abuse, it's pretty difficult for an outsider like me to intercede. And that boy really needs help of some kind—he's terrified if he hears so much as a raised voice. I can only imagine the nightmares he must still have after seeing his mom killed."

"Well, that clears things up." Connor's jaw clenched. "A scrawny, bandy rooster of a guy came in this afternoon. He was rude and demanding, and when I didn't have the right size gift box, he got pretty loud. He slammed the door on his way out."

"And that's all it takes for the poor kid." She slumped into one of the wrought-iron chairs by the front window. "I know he's living with a relative and that's what the county deems best, but how I wish I could give him even a year of a better life."

"At least he has a job here—and someone looking out for him."

Her heart warmed as she recalled the moment when she'd come back and found Connor sitting on the floor with Bobby while keeping up a flow of gentle, reassuring words. "Thank you, Connor, for what you did for him."

He shrugged, as if it had been nothing. But she knew in her very bones that he would be a good and loving father to his son; a good and loyal husband for someone.

She felt a twinge of regret at the thought.

She had to stay here and he would have to leave, so maintaining professional distance between them was the safest course. No doubt about it.

Yet at the end of the day, when Connor asked if she'd join him for supper over a campfire tomorrow night, to reciprocate for the dinner at her dad's house, her common sense flew out the window and she instantly said yes.

What was she thinking?

Chapter Eleven

Even sitting at his campfire that night, Connor couldn't get Bobby out of his mind.

The thought of what the boy had gone through still had the power to send a wave of nausea through Connor's midsection. He'd steered way clear of men like Bobby's father in prison—abusers who showed no remorse, only rage over being convicted…and who baldly proclaimed that they'd get their revenge once released.

If there was truly such a thing as prison justice—where abusers of children were handed mortal retribution by their peers—Connor sure hadn't seen it.

Which meant Bobby's father might live to be released someday. The thought was chilling.

When Keeley came out here tomorrow night for supper, he wanted to ask her more questions. Connor stoked his campfire and sent a shower of sparks spinning into the black-velvet sky, then looked up as a gray-haired man and two young boys strolled by, towels slung over their arms. He nodded at them. "Nice night."

"So far." The portly gentleman nodded and kept walking, but the boys stopped and stared at his fire.

"Grampa forgot wood for a fire," the younger one said

somberly. "So we can't have s'mores. And Charlie's mad 'cause we even gots the chocolate and marshmallows and everything."

His older brother gave him an elbow. "It's gonna rain anyway, stupid."

Their grandpa turned and gave the older one a stern look. "No name-calling. Remember? Now, what do you say to Kyle?"

Charlie stubbed a toe in the dirt and mumbled out an insincere "Sorry."

Connor rose and smiled down at the boys. "You know what? I bought too much wood today, and if we're getting more rain later, it will get too wet to use. Would you do me a favor and take some of it?"

"Really?" both boys said in unison.

Their grandfather hesitated. "I don't have my billfold on me right now."

"Forget it. Just go have some fun." He loaded each boy's proffered arms with wood and then handed more to the older man.

"I'll come by in the morning and settle up with you, promise. Thanks." The older fellow took a few steps then turned back. "I'm Bill, by the way. Bill Gordon. Be careful tonight. I heard on the radio about heavy storms north of here, and the forecasters say we've got sixty-percent chance of the same."

Connor glanced at the rocky bluff that rose high above the creek to the east, dimly lit by his flickering campfire. "You might want to set up camp on higher ground if you're down low. I think I'll do the same."

"We're good. My motor home is parked in a great spot." He waved and the three disappeared into the darkness, the high, youthful voices of the boys echoing off the bluffs as they chattered about campfires and marshmallows and a puppy waiting for them back at their campsite.

Picking up his supplies and moving higher along the bluffs didn't take Connor long with such minimal gear. In a half hour his tent was set up under a rocky outcropping he'd noticed earlier in the day, partially protected from the weather, with everything securely stowed. A good five feet higher than the bank of the stream where he'd been before, it ought to be safe enough.

Instead of starting a campfire, he turned on a couple of solar lanterns that he'd left outside all day to charge up in the sun. He settled down, leaned against the rock wall of the bluffs and smiled to himself, thinking of the two young boys who were probably tussling over those s'mores and the tending of the fire, and wearing their poor grandfather flat out.

But then the memories of Joshua's early years started coming back and Connor's amusement faded.

He'd been four when Connor went to prison, a bright-eyed chatterbox who wanted answers to a million questions and who never slowed down unless he was asleep. Even then, he tossed and turned, too busy in his dreams to stay tucked in.

Connor's own poignant dreams of that time often came tiptoeing into his thoughts this time of day, then stayed all night and kept him awake until dawn.

But the rain and wind had risen sharply during the past half hour, and maybe the staccato beat of rain and the rush of wind through the trees would make sleep come easier.

He climbed into the down sleeping bag in his tent and secured the exterior flap against the strengthening buffets of wind, then closed his eyes and hoped for the best.

It seemed like only minutes later when terrified screams filled the air.

Connor flew out his tent, grabbed one of the solar lanterns and held it high in the slashing rain driven nearly horizontal by the high winds.

Lightning razored through the sky, illuminating a roiling rush of water pouring through the grassy area where Connor had first set up camp. The water had to be ten, fifteen feet above the usual surface of Aspen Creek, and the flash flood had grabbed entire trees that were now bobbing past at a dizzying speed.

Picnic tables spun by, crashing against the rocks and then ricocheting back out into the raging flood.

Another terrified scream rent the air—closer now. Searching madly at his feet, Connor clawed at the ground for a coil of rope he'd left just outside his tent then raced down the rocky embankment below his campsite to the edge of the water and swung the lantern's beam through the darkness.

"Where are you?" he bellowed, knowing he could barely be heard above the roar of the water and crashing thunder overhead.

"Help! Help me!" a young voice screamed. "Please!"

Blinking away the rain, Connor swung his lamp again—and there was Kyle, desperately clinging to a picnic table caught in a logjam midstream with something sodden and lifeless caught in the crook of his elbow. A stuffed animal? Had he risked his life for that?

The tangle of uprooted trees was bouncing, swaying, in the onslaught of the rushing water. At any moment they could break free and rocket past, leaving the boy helpless—threatening to sweep him from his makeshift raft as they tumbled through the water. There'd be no hope for rescue then. *None.*

Even now, with the logjam at least twenty feet from shore, the deep, violently churning water made reaching the boy nearly impossible.

A slight figure in a yellow hooded rain jacket came running from the direction of the parking lot. *Keeley?*

"Connor—you've got to get out of here," she yelled above the wind. "The National Weather Service has issued flash-flood warnings and—"

"Can't," he yelled back. He lifted an arm and pointed at the water. "A kid is out there."

Her eyes widened in horror. "Can we get him?"

He pulled her close to yell in her ear. "Just go back to town and stay safe. And start praying."

"I'll pray, but I'm not leaving. You might need help."

The obstinate lift of her chin and her resolute expression told him he'd only waste precious time trying to argue.

Slipping and sliding in the mud, tripping over rocks and branches, he raced to the point on the bank closest to the logjam, with Keeley at his heels. From far upstream he could hear the boy's grandfather screaming Kyle's name.

At the water's edge he thrust the lantern into Keeley's hands.

"Okay, Kyle," he shouted into the screaming wind. "I'm here, and I'm going to get you out of there. Hang on and do not let go. Hear?"

His rope was nothing more than forty feet of limp white nylon—nothing like the stiff lariats he'd used to rope cattle most of his life. He quickly tied a slipknot at one end and formed a loop. "I'm going to throw this noose at you, kid. Grab it if you can, and hook it around your chest."

The boy stared at him, his eyes wide with terror. "I c-can't. I c-c-can't," he cried.

"You have to catch this, buddy." Connor tried once. Twice. Three times.

With each throw, the fierce wind whipped the rope downstream, nearly tangling on the bobbing branches and roots of the uprooted trees.

The entire mass jerked and shifted again. Jerked downstream a good ten feet.

"Help me!" Kyle screamed. "Please."

The picnic table under him bucked and pivoted. An edge slipped under a tree trunk, nearly upending before it wedged tight once more.

Connor froze. If the boy slipped off, he could be swept under those trees and drown.

"New plan," he shouted as he moved a dozen feet upstream, tied the end of the rope around the leg of a teeter-totter frame—galvanized pipe set in cement. *God, please let it hold. Help me.* "I'm coming for you. Hang tight."

He started to tie the other end of the rope around his waist. Keeley grabbed his arm and shook her head. "Let me go—I'm a strong swimmer. I've got a good chance of making it between all those branches. And I'm much lighter, so you can pull us in when I get him."

He shook his head. "Risk your life? Not a chance. Hold the lantern. Then guide us back in."

He took a short running start and dived as far into the raging flood as he could.

Instantly the violent force of the water sucked him deep into the icy blackness, obscuring his vision. His head hit a boulder at the bottom, sending a burst of pain and dizziness rocketing through him.

A wall of floodwater slammed into him, sending him downstream. Tumbling helplessly, he managed to struggle to the surface and take a strangled breath before the racing water threatened to pull him under again.

He slammed against something hard, rough, unforgiving. Another tree? He grabbed it, launched himself upward and hung on. In the dim light he saw Kyle just a few yards downstream.

The sound of sirens wailed in the distance as he pushed

away and swam hard to reach the boy. "Okay, k-kid," he sputtered as a wave of water slammed into his face. "I've got a rope and I need you to help me get it around your chest. Let that stuffed animal go, Kyle—"

"No," the kid screamed, clutching it tighter under one arm. He was pale as flour, his teeth chattering. "Don't make me!"

Connor blinked the water from his eyes and realized the boy held a weakly shivering puppy.

Gripping a tree branch with one hand, Connor worked one-handed at the knot at his waist with numb, icy fingers. After three tries he managed to get it around Kyle's chest and tied a quick bowline knot.

Seconds later the logjam of trees broke free with an unearthly shriek and disappeared into the darkness, taking Kyle's picnic table with them.

Kyle went under water but Connor reeled him in, sputtering and coughing.

Connor spit out a mouthful of filthy water. He hooked an arm around the boy and his pup, and let the current drag them downstream until the rope grew taut with an abrupt jerk.

It held fast. *Thank You, Lord.*

And then Keeley was hauling on the rope, trying to pull them back in.

Battling the current, they swung like a pendulum, closer to the bank as she took up the slack. What had been a quiet little creek was too deep to touch bottom and the racing current clawed at them as he fought to reach the shore.

Cold and exhaustion seeped through Connor's muscles, making each effort slower. Weaker.

He struggled harder. "Don't worry, kid—almost there."

Like voices in a dream, he heard the sound of Keeley

shouting. Felt her superhuman, adrenaline-charged efforts to bring them in to safety.

Now he saw distant lights flashing through the darkness.

And then somehow they hit the rocks along the shore and Kyle was lifted from his arms.

Coughing, Connor staggered to higher ground and when his legs wobbled he dropped, his forehead on his upraised knees. Someone draped a blanket over his shoulders.

Flashlights swung through the area as more people arrived and milled around. From the depths of his foggy awareness he heard an old man crying.

Oh, God. Please, no. Had the boy drowned in his arms, even as they were trying to escape the river? Connor's heart clenched on a wave of searing grief. *Please, please. Let him be okay. Please...*

Chapter Twelve

Keeley hurried into the emergency room at the tiny Aspen Creek hospital, her heart in her throat.

Tom Benson, one of the regular ushers at church, sat behind the admittance desk and looked up. "Quite a night, eh?"

Her pulse pounding, she brushed all pleasantries aside. "I'm here for Connor Rafferty. The EMTs brought him here but I couldn't keep up with them on the highway. Is he okay?"

Tom waved her toward the waiting room. "We wanted to put him on a gurney and take him into the ER, but he's refusing to be seen. I hear he just wants to go home."

Her hand at her throat, she stared at him. "But is he *okay*?"

Tom shrugged. "Ask him—he's in the waiting room. He hasn't been the most cooperative patient we've ever had, believe me. But he has a head injury, and if he wants to risk keeling over, that's his right."

"Head injury?" Her heart in her throat, she spun around and headed for the waiting room around the corner, where she found a half dozen dazed people wrapped in blankets, looking shell-shocked.

Connor sat by himself in the corner, his head leaning back against the wall. Weariness etched his face. A jagged cut from his temple to the corner of his jaw still seeped blood; his hands were covered with scrapes and several deeper cuts.

His dark hair appeared matted on one side—probably even more blood.

She hurried to his side and sank into the chair next to him. "I'd just gone to bed when I heard the sirens go off in town, and then I heard about the flash flood on the radio. I came as fast as I could. Are you all right?"

He slid a glance at her, nodded faintly, then closed his eyes again.

She glanced around the room and realized that others were in the same shape. Exhausted, with bruises and lacerations. "From the looks of everyone, this could have been a terrible tragedy."

A haggard man with gray hair appeared in the doorway, his arm wrapped tightly around the shoulders of a dazed, muddy boy of maybe nine or ten. They both walked into the room and headed straight for Connor. The man extended a hand.

When Connor stood to accept his handshake the man turned it into a bear hug. Then he enveloped Keeley in a hug, as well.

He stepped back with tears in his eyes. "I can never, ever, repay you for what you did tonight."

"Right place, right time," Connor said. "I'm just glad I was there and that Keeley came to help."

"I didn't stop praying from the moment Kyle raced off to get his puppy out of the creek." The man's voice broke and he shook his head slowly, his eyes closed at the painful memory. "When that flash flood hit and they disappeared, I figured I'd never see either of them alive again. You were the answer to my prayers."

Connor glanced at Keeley. "This is Bill Gordon. He and his grandsons were camping, too." Connor turned back to the older man. "Will Kyle be all right?"

Bill clapped Connor on the shoulder and sank wearily into the chair at Connor's other side. His younger grandson stretched out on the floor. "The docs tell me he'll be fine. He's off at Radiology right now to check his left arm, and they'll probably keep him overnight. And the puppy is fine. It's staying at a vet clinic for a day or two. What about you?"

"I was just waiting for a ride back to my campsite." Connor's laugh held a rueful note. "Usually I'd hike, but after tonight I feel a little lazy."

"Exhausted is more like it." The man reared back in his chair and studied Connor. "The nurses didn't even clean you up a little? Looks like you could use a few stitches."

"I used to rodeo and this is nothing, believe me. My tent and a good night's sleep is all I need."

Bill frowned. "They didn't tell you?"

"About what?"

"How bad it was. The flood rose clear up to the windows in my motor home, and the entire lower campground was swept clean. Anything you had out there is long gone into the St. Croix and probably halfway down the Mississippi by now."

Already pale and drawn, Connor sagged into his chair, and Keeley wanted to wrap an arm around him. But she'd seen him flinch during Bill's grateful hug and now she wondered just how badly he'd been hurt.

"I think we should have the docs look you over," she murmured.

He shook his head. "Not necessary."

"Because of the cost?" she asked quietly.

When he didn't answer, Bill leaned forward. "Ma'am, go tell the nurses this man hasn't yet been seen. He saved my grandson's life, and whatever it costs, I'll foot the bill. And if he needs a place to stay, I'll figure that out, too. I owe him more than I can ever repay."

It was three in the morning before the doctors released Connor after an exam, X-rays, an MRI of his chest and head, and twelve sutures.

Bill had long since talked to the billing department about Connor's expenses and offered to pay for a hotel room, as well, then had taken his younger grandson home.

Keeley studied Connor's face as the nurses walked him out of the ER entrance to her SUV. Once they were on the road, she glanced at him again before returning her attention to the highway.

"By tomorrow, you're going to look like you were in a fight and lost," she teased. "You'll be moving around like someone old as Methuselah."

He leaned his head against the headrest. "Probably."

"I'm not taking you to a hotel, by the way. The discharge instructions say you should be under observation for twenty-four hours because of that concussion, so I'm taking you to Dad's house and I'll stay there, too."

He gave her a sidelong look then closed his eyes. "That's not necessary. It's just more bother for you."

"Actually, I've been thinking."

"Should I be worried? I'm not being fired, am I?"

She laughed, relieved that he felt good enough to tease her back. "Fire a local hero? Not on your life. You'll be front-page news in the next issue of the *Aspen Herald*."

He groaned. "Not what I want to hear."

"But this ought to put Millie and her gossipy friends

in their place. They were reveling in their juicy news and now you've gone and saved a little boy *and* his puppy." She glanced at him again when he didn't respond. He looked so pale and drawn in the faint light of the dashboard that she wondered if he should have been kept in the hospital overnight. "Are you all right? Did the doc give you anything for pain?"

"No."

"Is there anything you can take? Should we go back? I can't believe they didn't give you something."

"Just local anesthetic during the sutures. Tylenol would be okay but I don't need it."

"No need to be all macho with me," she said. "If you want to tough it out, that's your choice. But I can well imagine what you'll feel like in the morning with all of those cuts, bruises and a cracked rib. Why didn't they put some sort of compression bandage on you? That's what I got as a kid when I fell off the monkey bars."

He shot a dry look at her. "That's old school. Now they fear suppressing your deep breathing and the risk of pneumonia. Anyway, this isn't my first time. I think most of my ribs have been cracked at some time or other."

"Rodeo?"

He nodded. "So it's no big deal."

"I disagree. It still must hurt." She pulled to a stop in front of Dad's house and hurried around the SUV to open his door. "Ready?"

He surveyed the darkened house. "This is going to wake your dad up in the middle of the night. Does he even know we're coming?"

"No," she admitted. "It was too late to call."

"He'll think we're burglars. Is he armed, by any chance?"

"No guns. And, anyway, he sleeps in a bedroom upstairs and takes his hearing aids out at night, so he'll never know we've arrived, and the dog knows both of us, so he won't bark… I hope. I'm putting you in a small guest room on the main floor."

Connor eased out of the vehicle, one arm gingerly wrapped around his ribs.

"Right. This is no big deal," she said dryly. "Do you want me to help you up to the house?"

"Thanks, but I've got this." He slowly followed her up the long cement sidewalk to the porch, then white-knuckled the banister as he eased up the steps.

Once she got him to the guest room, she flipped on the light by the queen-size bed and turned down the colorful patchwork quilt. "I'll be back in a second."

In the hall bathroom she found a new toothbrush and an unopened travel-size toothpaste in one of the drawers and set them on the counter with a set of fresh towels.

After a moment's thought, she brought a cup of water and a bottle of Tylenol to place on the bedside table. "Here you go—in case you find it's going to be a hard night. The bathroom is two doors down, and I set out fresh towels for you. I'll be peeking in to check on you every two hours, just as the nurse said."

The soft light of the bedside lamp shadowed the lean planes and hollows of his face; his five o'clock shadow and unruly hair made her think of the swashbuckling pirates in some novels she'd recently read.

Despite the weariness etched in his face, he was still more appealing than anyone she'd ever met, but today she'd seen more than just superficial good looks.

He was her real-life hero.

Something shifted in her heart, breaking away some of the protective walls she'd so carefully erected over the years.

"Sleep well," she whispered, reaching up to rest a gentle

hand against his uninjured cheek. "If you need anything, just call my name. I'll be down the hall."

She started to turn away but he caught her hand and gently pulled her back. Goose bumps raced up her arm at his touch.

"Don't go," he whispered.

When their gazes locked she felt transfixed—unable to look away from the depth of emotion she saw in his eyes. She licked her suddenly dry lips. "Is…is there something else you need?"

His mouth kicked up a little at one corner, deepening the dimple on that side, and she blushed a little at the possible double meaning of her words.

"I just want to thank you, Keeley, for everything you've done."

She glanced around the bedroom then managed a small smile, trying to ignore the hint of farewell in his words. "This guest room was empty. I'm sure Dad won't mind."

"I didn't just mean the room." He rubbed his thumb against the back of her hand, sending warmth through her veins and straight to her heart. "When I was first released, I had no idea what to expect from people on the outside. You've given me back my self-respect, and the feeling that maybe I really do have a chance after all."

"I know you do. I have no doubt at all." She gave him her most confident smile. "But now I'd better let you get some sleep. It's been a long day."

Minutes later she set her smartphone alarm for two hours and snuggled under an afghan on the sofa in the family room, but sleep eluded her. Instead, an endless loop of thoughts about Connor kept cycling in her head.

He could have made a halfhearted rescue attempt and then given up to keep himself safe, but he'd totally risked his life for a stranger and had protected a puppy with his life, as well. What man would do that? Yet afterward, his only concerns had been about their welfare, and he'd firmly discounted his heroics to anyone who praised him.

With each passing day she'd been drawn to him a little more. And who wouldn't be?

Despite his protestations about being ill-suited to working at the store, he was good with the customers and kept busy with fix-it projects when none were around. He hadn't complained once—not about his rough living conditions at the campground, not about the more difficult shoppers who came into the store.

But more than that, he'd been truly concerned about Bobby and he'd been patient and kind to her difficult father. Even crotchety old Bart liked him, and that dog didn't like anyone but her dad.

Still, as her lingering doubts about Connor faded away, one truth remained.

No matter how kind or honest or charming he was… no matter how much her feelings might grow, there was no point in hoping for anything more.

He'd drifted into her life unexpectedly and within weeks he'd be gone—off to find his son and reestablish his life. And to do that, he'd need to return to the world he knew best—ranching or the rodeo circuit, somewhere out West.

A Wisconsin tourist town like Aspen Creek would have nothing to offer a man like him.

Chapter Thirteen

Though he hadn't wanted to admit it to the nurses or anyone else, Connor had known this morning was going to be a bear. His muscles ached and his head still throbbed, and he hadn't even been sure where he was during the first foggy moments of awakening after a fitful night of sleep.

Instead of a sleeping bag and thin foam mat on hard ground, this was a comfortable bed, with warm blankets. The rosy blush of dawn slipping through the edges of the curtains softly lit the antique furnishings and stained-glass lamps on the dresser and bedside table.

He closed his eyes, savoring the comforts of a real home for the first time in years. Then he slowly sat up, despite the muscles screaming in protest, and reached for the damp jeans, socks and shirt he'd draped over a chair.

Sometime during the early morning hours Keeley must have washed and dried them, for now they were clean and neatly folded on the dresser. Keeley and he had arrived here after three in morning, so had she got any sleep at all? Surprised and grateful, he pulled on his clothes, shoved his damp wallet in his pocket and stepped into the hallway.

The house was quiet, with no breakfast aromas emanating from the kitchen, so everyone else was probably asleep.

The possibility of making a much-needed cup of coffee drew him down the hall and through an archway into a formal living room he hadn't seen when he'd been here for supper. It was filled with stiff, uncomfortable-looking, gilt-and-white furnishings, upholstered in the color of fresh cream.

He paused and stared for a moment, imagining what he and his brothers would have done to a room like this during their mud-and-sticky-fingers childhood days. Was this how Keeley had been raised—in a grand place where she couldn't sit on the furniture or play with childhood abandon? How had she turned out to be so easygoing? So *normal*?

Through the next archway he could see a more familiar area—the family room, where Keeley's dad watched television. The massive, dark-paneled room was lined with bookshelves and filled with heavy leather furniture. He continued on toward the kitchen, less comfortable about his mission with each step—feeling more like a prowler than a guest.

If he suddenly met up with Paul North, he sincerely hoped he wouldn't give the poor man a heart attack.

Something rustled at the far end of the family room and he stilled.

"I thought you would sleep later," Keeley murmured. Setting aside an afghan, she rose from a pillowy, burgundy-leather sofa. "You sure tossed and turned a lot last night. Every time I checked on you, you were restless."

He laughed. "I guess I must sleep better outside."

"How are you this morning?"

"Good—just in search of some coffee. Does your dad keep any on hand?"

She led the way into a dazzling white kitchen with stainless-steel appliances, flipped on the lights and headed for the Keurig at the end of the granite counter. "Name your flavor and we probably have it."

"Anything with caffeine." While the machine gurgled, he glanced around the kitchen. Just as it had been before, it was beautiful but stark, and lacking any sort of homey details such as the ones he remembered from every other home he'd ever seen. Not so much as a pot holder or a kitchen towel was in view.

"This place is spotless," he murmured. "I think you could do surgery on the counters."

"Almost. I try to cook for the two of us when I can, and make enough for leftovers he can reheat. Or he nukes those healthy frozen dinners. But no matter what, Dad wants this place tidy before he goes to bed." She handed Connor a steaming mug. "This is French vanilla. If you don't like it, I can make something else."

He took a sip of the rich, dark brew. "Perfect."

"I agree with you, though. This kitchen is awfully Spartan, but that's what Dad likes, so that's what he has." She went to the refrigerator and opened the door wide. "What do you want for breakfast? I can make any kind of eggs you want, with bacon or sausage. And there's whole wheat or sourdough for toast."

"Don't go to any work for me. I figure I'd better get out and buy a tent, some clothes and supplies. I can grab some breakfast on the way."

"About those supplies… I'm guessing that it's going to be a pretty hefty bill, if you're replacing everything you lost. Right?"

He shrugged. "I don't have much choice."

She pulled a loaf of bread from a cupboard and a tub of margarine from the fridge, and put two slices of bread in the toaster.

She turned back to him, her eyes sparkling. "Actually,

I have a plan. It will save you a lot of money and it will help me out. A lot. And it will actually give you a chance to earn more money while you're here. Sound good?"

He gave her a wary look. "Too good."

"Here's the deal." She looked over his shoulder toward the door then lowered her voice.

"My dad refuses to let anyone else help him except for me—and that's only sometimes. He's mostly too proud to accept any assistance, and too stubborn to admit it. Sometimes I think he'd rather die than lose his independence."

"Sounds like my grandpa back in Texas."

The toast popped up. She buttered the slices and put them on a plate by Connor's mug, and retrieved a jar of raspberry jam from the fridge for him. "Well… I've tried to hire a housekeeper who could also sort of watch over him, but he would have none of that. Same with a visiting county caregiver. I even offered to move in, just so someone would be around at night, but we're like oil and water and he refused." Her mouth tilted into a wry smile. "Which was probably the best thing all around."

"If you're suggesting I stay here, I think his answer would be the same, don't you?"

"Maybe not. Your campsite was wiped out and Dad has four empty bedrooms in this house plus three little rental cabins in the back, which are also empty. He'd simply be doing you a favor."

Connor shook his head. "I couldn't impose like that."

"But it wouldn't be an imposition at all. He has empty rooms, you need a place to stay. A perfect match. And it would be free rent—if you could just look in on him now and then, and maybe help him mow. It would be such peace of mind knowing someone was here in case anything happened."

"You really think he'd agree? I sort of doubt it. And, anyway, I should be on the road in a few weeks."

"True, but the great part is that this would ease Dad into the idea of having someone around." She tapped a forefinger on her lips, thinking. "I'd just have to make sure I approached him the right way."

"Approached *what* the right way?"

They both turned toward the door at the accusatory sound of Paul's voice, and Keeley paled. "Um, good morning, Dad."

"What are you doing here at this hour?" Paul's eyes narrowed on Connor. Then his icy gaze slid over to Keeley. "You were both here overnight, in my house?"

Keeley visibly stiffened. "For Pete's sake, Dad. Give me a little credit. A flash flood wiped out the campground last night—including everything Connor owned. He saved a little boy from drowning, but then he ended up in the emergency room himself until three this morning. He had nowhere else to go, and the doctor's orders were that someone needed to check on him regularly because he has a concussion. So I brought him here. I was on the sofa in the den, and I gave Connor the downstairs guest room."

Paul's gaze didn't thaw. "Then what's this about approaching me the right way? What is it you're after—money?"

"No, Dad." Keeley set her jaw. "He lost *everything*. He doesn't have a place to stay and you can easily help him out. Anyway, he'll only be in town a couple weeks more, so it's not like he can rent an apartment somewhere. With tourist season starting, a hotel or B and B for that long would cost a fortune."

"Humph." Paul shuffled over to the coffeemaker and made himself a cup, then turned to face them.

"We surely wouldn't charge him," she continued. "But

for the short time he's here—in one of the little cabins and out of your way—he could mow or help with some little jobs around the house. You're always complaining about the jiggly lock set on the front door."

Paul glowered at her. "Just a few weeks?"

"Right."

His gaze raked Connor head to toe. "No alcohol. No parties. No carousing. No loud music."

Connor reined in the temptation to laugh. "No, sir. No problem at all."

The sun was setting as Connor lugged the last storage box out of Cabin 3 and added it to the stack headed for one of the other cabins, then stepped back inside. "Anything else?"

"Done, and after a busy day at the store plus this, I'm ready to call it quits." Keeley set aside her dust cloth, rested her hands on her hips and studied his bruised and battered face. "I regret even asking if you could help me with all of this. How are those sutures feeling? And your concussion?"

"The Tylenol did help," he admitted with a rueful laugh. "But I think I'm ready to call it a day, too."

"At least you'll have a decent place to stay." She surveyed the cabin one more time, looking for anything they might have forgotten. "I don't suppose you've ever watched HGTV."

"What?"

"It's the only show I watch, other than public television. They show houses being renovated and people shopping for homes. Everyone seems focused on 'open concept' layouts and 'sight lines' so you can see several rooms at once." She grinned. "I think this cabin is a great example—except it's the size of a postage stamp."

"Whatever this is called, it looks fine to me. I'm just happy to have a roof."

"And one that's in good condition. But the floors sure need to be redone." She ran a hand over the yellow laminate counter in the kitchen, guessing that it dated from the 1970s. "And this would need replacing if the cabins were ever put into regular use."

"If you make a list, I can work on it during the evenings."

"That would be nice. Looking at this place sure makes me feel nostalgic. My mom always rented out the cabins by the week throughout tourist season, and I remember hoping that there'd be kids my age, now and then."

The cabin was basically one room, with a sofa and TV at one end and a tiny kitchen at the other, all done in Northwoods-style pine paneling, with pine flooring and a scattering of handmade rugs. At the far side, there was a single, small bedroom and adjoining bathroom. Now that the cabin had been cleaned, dustcovers removed from the furniture, bed made and towels hung, it looked ready for use.

"This is actually rather charming," she mused. "In a retro sort of way. Maybe we should start renting the cabins again. Dad couldn't handle it and I don't have the time, but I could hire someone in the neighborhood to handle the housekeeping and guests. Dad might enjoy seeing different people come and go. I want to apologize for his behavior this morning, by the way. He had no business assuming the worst about us being here."

Connor shrugged. "He's a father. If I had a daughter, I'd probably be a hundred times worse."

"I also want to apologize about him giving you the third degree this morning. I hardly think you'd be the wild party type."

He tipped his head in silent acknowledgment. "During my college and early rodeo days, those would have been valid warnings. Now, not so much. But that's okay. He has a right to protect his property and he should be up-front about it."

"I hope you feel as forgiving after you've been living here for a few days. He isn't always the most patient man and he might be out here overseeing any project you start."

"Well, my time is yours, until my truck is done. Just tell me what needs to be done."

"Better be careful. Before long I'll have you so busy that you'll forget about moving on." She grinned at him, then took a last glance at the results of their hard work and handed him the cabin key. "Now you can move in—except that you have nothing to put away. We need to get you to Walmart for some clothes. There are all sorts of boutiques and fancy-pants stores in town, but I'm afraid that's the only place in town for guy things like jeans."

"And everything else I need, really. Some groceries and one of their prepaid smartphones. I'll need it for the GPS while traveling and the internet until I can get a computer."

"I can give you your first four days' pay today. Also an advance, if you need it."

"Thank you," he said quietly.

The warmth and gratitude in his eyes took her aback, so she gave him a breezy smile to lighten the moment as she opened the front door. "No problem at all."

"No—I really mean it."

He rested a hand on her shoulder as he spoke and she stilled, unable to take another step as gentle warmth and something deeper than that seemed to travel straight to her heart…though she suspected he affected most women under the age of ninety the same way. What woman could possibly be immune to such a good-looking and charisma-laden cowboy?

His easy Texas drawl and innate Southern manners just added to the lethal appeal that was made all the more entrancing because he didn't seem to be aware of the impact it caused.

"It seems like a lifetime ago since I was around anyone as thoughtful and caring as you are," he continued. "And I don't think anyone around here even realizes how special you are."

"I, um…" Flustered, she didn't know what to say. Especially because she sensed he wanted to kiss her, and *that* sent her pulse into overdrive.

She'd had that private fantasy ever since he'd first appeared in her store—so tall and dark and utterly handsome, though now it was the man inside who drew her.

"Thank you. For everything you've done for me…and Josh." Their gazes locked. "It's funny. I've spent a lot of years being angry at the Almighty, thinking He never cared enough to answer my prayers. But now I realize He has all along. He brought me to you."

Chapter Fourteen

Connor had hoped Keeley was kidding when she talked about the flash flood being first-page news in the *Aspen Herald.*

The paper clutched in Paul's hand on Thursday evening proved otherwise.

During the tense moments after pulling Kyle through the water to safety and afterward, among the milling crowd of EMTs, deputies and shell-shocked campers, Connor hadn't been aware of anyone taking photos.

But there they were—front page.

Connor in the water, lifting Kyle up to the waiting arms of a deputy, the boy's grandfather right behind him with a distraught expression.

Connor cradling the shivering puppy before handing him to someone else.

A photo taken through the back door of the First Response Vehicle, showing an EMT hovering over the child, who lay on the gurney inside with an IV bag hanging above him.

"I guess you did have quite a night on Tuesday," Paul said with a grudging look of admiration. "Given who you rescued, this will probably make the papers in Madison and the Twin Cities."

"Kyle? Nice kid."

"His dad is a state senator, and one of the top picks to run for president the next time around. The family is loaded, so I hear."

Connor shot a sideways glance at him. "I had no idea."

"Keeley says the grandfather insisted on paying your medical bills at the ER, and that you were planning on paying him back. Guess you don't have to worry about that now, eh?"

"It makes no difference."

Paul's eyebrows lifted. "They don't need the money. And do you even have any?"

The old guy was blunt—Connor had to give him that. "It'll take a while. I need to find a job and get settled, and try to get my son back. But that's a debt I'll owe."

Paul took his measure with a long, thoughtful look. Then he handed over the newspaper. "This is an extra copy. I thought you might want it. And you might want to read the article. For better or worse, they've written a fair amount about you and it may or may not be accurate. People can research anyone on Google these days, but is it true? Not always."

Connor sighed. "Now I don't think I want to read it, honestly. But thanks."

Settling on the wrought-iron bench in front of Cabin 3, with his old dog at his feet, Paul laid the paper aside and watched Connor paint the white trim around the front door. "Is it true you came from one of the biggest ranches in north Texas?"

Connor concentrated on finishing another long section of the trim, then dipped his brush in the paint can and continued painting. "One of them, I guess."

"And that you were in the running at the PRCA Championships in saddle broncs before getting yourself arrested?"

Connor sighed. "The rodeo part is true, but I didn't 'get myself arrested.' I had nothing to do with it. Nothing. That was a series of errors that never should have happened."

"All that money and success, yet here you are, working for my daughter. Traveling on a shoestring across the country. I don't get it. Why don't you hit up your family for the money then hire an investigator and a good lawyer to get your son back? Or go back to rodeo and earn the money?"

"For someone who was so grumpy and silent when we first met, you're proving to be remarkably talkative," Connor said dryly.

Paul's eyes narrowed and Connor wondered if he'd gone too far.

But then the old man tipped his head back and laughed. "True, but you're the most interesting thing to come along around here in quite a while. And I'm curious."

"My dad was furious when I went on the rodeo circuit after college. After a few spectacular arguments, he quit talking to me." Connor eyed the trim, caught an errant drip and continued painting. "During our last conversation, he informed me that my brothers would be taking over the ranch and not to bother about coming home."

"Shame on him."

"As for rodeo, I've reached the tipping point, because bronc riding is a younger man's sport. Even if I wanted to, I've lost out on too many years to make a comeback and reach the top again."

"Surely you don't plan on a career as a store clerk."

"Right now, I'm just grateful I can make money to pay for my truck repairs. But after this, I'll be open to any career that will help me raise my son."

Paul pursed his lips, his gaze fastened on the two apple

trees in his backyard that were beginning to bloom. "So what are your skills?"

"Cattle ranching. Breeding and training horses. I have a degree in ranch management, so I could work in a county extension office or be a sales rep for some type of agricultural company, but ranch management would be my choice."

"Guess there wouldn't be much of that around here."

"Nope. Which is why I need to head back to Montana or Texas." Connor finished the last section of trim on the window, backed up to study his handiwork and laid the brush aside on the upturned lid of the paint can. "The sooner I can get things settled with Joshua and move west, the better it will be."

The sooner I can get things settled with Joshua and move west, the better it will be.

Keeley paused as she crossed the backyard toward Connor's cabin, his words sinking into her flesh like tiny darts of disappointment.

Of course, it wasn't a surprise. She hadn't ever expected him to stay in town long term. His goal of leaving Aspen Creek had been crystal clear from day one—and it was the polar opposite of her own.

Yet…this past week she'd truly enjoyed his company and their conversations. Being with him had been like peeling back layers—finding out more about him every day. Good things. Admirable things.

Qualities she hadn't found in the men she had occasionally dated over the past few years. And when he left town, she suspected it would be a long time before she found another man like him. Maybe never.

Like right now—was Dad actually *laughing*? Who had ever engaged her dad in conversation like Connor could?

Even Todd—a deputy who ought to be a take-charge, brave sort of guy—usually managed only a few words, then backed off in the face of Dad's irascible temperament.

She heaved a sigh as she halted in front of the cabin. "Hey, guys. Sorry I'm late. I've got supper waiting on the counter if you want to come inside."

Connor dropped his paintbrush in a plastic pail of water and hammered the lid back on the paint can at his feet. "So what do you think? Like the colors?"

She'd asked him to spend the day painting rather than come into the store, figuring he could just take it easy and not overstress his sore ribs. But instead of dabbling at the project, he'd finished the entire cabin.

The dark blue blended into the surrounding pines like a cool, dark shadow, while the crisp white trim and the gingerbread detailing along the eaves were as fresh as starched-white lace. "Beautiful. You've done a great job."

"One down, two cabins to go."

"You might as well eat supper with us," Paul muttered as he rose to his feet and headed for the house, snapping his fingers for Bart to follow.

Bart watched him go, then dropped at Connor's feet.

"I know you bought supplies when we went to Walmart, but you will join us, won't you? Might as well," Keeley said with a smile. "I made lasagna and there's way too much for the two of us."

Connor surveyed his paint-splattered hands. "I usually run in the evening, but since I'm not quite up to that, I want to at least go for a walk before the sun goes down. And I've chili in the Crock-Pot. Maybe another time? But thanks all the same."

After walking a couple of miles out of town on a gravel country road, Connor's sore muscles began to ache and his nagging headache began to pound, so he turned back for the city limits and sauntered down the Main Street sidewalk past Keeley's store.

It was after six o'clock and everything was now closed, but pennants advertising the Aspen Creek Antique Walk swooped over Main at every street corner. Each of the businesses had placed colorful signs in its front window promising great sales, plus posters advertising family activities and bands playing at the fairgrounds throughout the weekend.

Tours of some of the grand old homes in town and horse-drawn carriage rides up and down Main were offered, as well as golf and tennis tournaments out at the public golf course.

He lingered in front of a florist shop and studied the array of flowering plants and, in a cooler visible from the sidewalk, some colorful floral arrangements. He had no idea what any of them were, but he found himself wondering which one Keeley would like the most.

Not that he had the extra money right now. That trip to the store this morning had eaten up his earnings for the first four days here, and he still needed to pay for his truck repairs.

But she was a woman who deserved flowers. Deserved a pretty home and a good husband who could provide for her well, so she wouldn't have to work so hard.

He didn't fit the bill on any score.

That was why he had declined her dinner offer, and why he was going to be more careful about keeping his distance in the future.

With his troubling prison background, a vindictive ex-wife, a son to raise and no clear career options in sight, the best thing he could do for Keeley would be to leave town... no matter how drawn he was to her.

He turned away from the store and walked back to his

temporary home, where he found a note on the table tucked under a mason jar filled with yellow, red and white flowers clearly picked from one of the gardens in the backyard.

The irony didn't escape him.

While he'd been looking through the florist shop window with empty pockets, she'd gone ahead and left him a note and a cheery bouquet that she'd picked herself.

> Connor—hope you don't mind that I stopped in. There's a plate of lasagna plus some garlic bread and romaine salad in your fridge, and a plate of brownies on the counter. It will all keep if you don't want it tonight.
>
> Tomorrow is a big day at the store. See you at 10!
>
> Thanks,
> Keeley.

The aroma of buttery garlic bread, rich meat sauce, fresh Parmesan and mozzarella wafted from the refrigerator when he opened the door. His pot of chili didn't even come close to the promise of such sensory pleasure.

When had he ever known someone like her?

His mother had walked out on her family and had rarely kept contact with her grieving kids. His own wife had paid little attention to her wedding vows. But Keeley was so different from the other women in his life—resolved to care for her obstinate father despite his protests, determined to shelter waifs, be they stray cats or troubled teens. She'd even taken in an ex-con like him.

Connor was glad his truck would be done in a few weeks, so he could be on his way.

Because the longer he stayed, the harder it would be to leave.

Chapter Fifteen

Friday dawned bright and sunny, with the streets already filling with tourist traffic and the promise of a successful weekend.

Red was scowling at the front door when Keeley unlocked it. "Is Connor here?"

"Um, just a minute." She went to the storeroom, where he was unpacking and price-stickering Wisconsin-themed Christmas ornaments, and waved for him to come up front.

Red cleared his throat. "You know that truck of yours? The problem ain't what I thought."

Connor jammed his thumbs in his jeans' pockets. "And?"

"I'd hoped it was the tranny, but you've got a bigger problem. Had the truck long?"

"No...just a couple weeks."

"That's what I thought." Red winked. "I'd heard you've been out of circulation for a while. Must have been quite an exper—"

"Red." Keeley interrupted him with a warning look. "About the truck?"

"Oh, yeah. Well, I've been real busy and didn't have time to take a good look till this morning. Wish I had—

’cause I coulda ordered parts by now if you really want to fix it.”

Connor’s jaw clenched. “What’s wrong?”

“Cracked engine block. The best fix is to go ahead and replace the engine.” Red dug in his pockets and withdrew a scrap of paper. “You’ve got a Number 53 engine block that’s known for this problem. Come down to the shop, if you want to see the damage yourself. Then you can Google your options.”

“It ran perfectly when I test-drove it.”

“I’m sure it did—for a while. Someone tried to repair the crack with a J-B weld, but that’s usually a temporary fix because of the wall thickness there. Eventually they crack again.”

“So the options are…?”

“A new engine block or a decent used one from a salvage yard. Or just sell the truck to a junkyard for salvage and buy something else.”

“If you repaired it, could I get three or four thousand miles out of it?”

“It’s already been repaired at least once, so I doubt it. And if I can’t guarantee my work, I won’t do it.” Red shrugged. “You might find someone else who’ll fix it, but I figure you’d be throwing that money away.”

“What would a used engine cost?”

“A fraction of the cost of a new one. I’m guessing maybe $700 to $1,200 plus shipping costs—unless I can find one nearby and can go pick it up myself. I’ll start looking, if that’s the way you want to go.”

“And installation?”

“Labor, fluids, miscellaneous parts…rough estimate, maybe $700.” Red scratched his chin, thinking. “I’ll treat you fair. Though once I tear into the truck, I might find other problems.”

From his bleak expression Connor was probably visualizing his plans to leave within two weeks going up in smoke. "That's almost what I paid for the truck back in Montana."

"I don't care if you decide to fix it or junk it." Red shrugged. "But it's gonna take a while to find the parts, so if you're in any kind of hurry, the quicker you decide, the better."

Keeley glanced between the two men. "I know nothing about cars, but if that truck was yours, what would you do?"

"I'd go through it to check for other major problems, to see if it's even worth doing the engine." Red took off his grease-stained Wisconsin Badgers ball cap and scratched his head. "If it is, then I'd hunt for a low-mileage, used engine in good shape. That way, it could be back on the road for under two grand and be driven for years. For the same amount you might find a used car, but I can guar-un-tee at that price you'll be buying someone else's problems and would soon be spending a lot of money on that one."

Glancing over his shoulder at the poster-size calendar on the wall, Connor hesitated then looked at Keeley. "Could you use me for a few weeks?"

"Of course. I'll always need an employee, and right now you're it," she said fervently. "I have no other prospects at the moment. So however long you need to be in town is fine with me."

"Thanks."

She bit her lower lip. "But as much as I appreciate you being here, have you thought about flying? It would sure be faster."

"I did do some checking on flights, but if I flew, last-minute tickets would cost as much as fixing my engine. Then I'd need to buy or lease a vehicle once I got to Detroit so I could search for Marsha, then try to find a lawyer. I have no idea how many meetings it will take to work everything out."

"True. Plus any court dates, and seeing Josh as much as you can. I wasn't thinking."

"It could be several weeks or even longer, while I try to regain shared custody. So I'm better off waiting for my truck." He looked at Red. "I'll go with a used engine. Any idea how long it will take to get the truck running?"

He rubbed his chin. "Depends on when I can find the right engine, when it can be shipped and then when I can fit in the installation once it arrives. A couple weeks—maybe longer. No guarantees."

Keeley met Connor's eyes after Red left. "That's a lot of maybes. Have you ever had anything like this done in the past?"

"Replace an engine? Not any of mine, but I watched a few times when I was a kid. My dad and the foreman always did it. When you're isolated in Texas ranch country, you learn to do a lot of things on your own."

"So you think this will go well? I mean, Red's a great guy but—"

The bells over the front door jangled and Todd walked in, his gray uniform starched and pressed, his service belt highly polished. He nodded at Keeley but zeroed in on Connor with laser-like intensity.

"So how are things going for you here, now that you're a big hero and all?"

"Todd," Keeley gasped at his sharp tone. "What has gotten into you?"

"Could be a matter of some thefts in town. Four, to be exact, and all since your friend came to town." Todd looked up at Connor and stabbed a pudgy forefinger at his chest.

"Colson's Menswear, Benson's Gifts, Diana's Boutique and Main Street Florist Shop. So far."

"It wasn't me," Connor said quietly.

"Good grief, Todd." Keeley threw her hands up in disgust. "Tell me what a man like Connor could possibly want in stores like those."

"That isn't the point."

She propped her hands on her hips and glared at the deputy. "Then what is? And tell me—were these thefts breaking and entering, or were they shoplifting? We always have trouble with shoplifting when the tourists start coming into town."

"The point is that I need to get to the bottom of this, fast. If the newspaper gets wind of a thief working in town, it would be headline news and could hurt our big tourist weekends. People won't feel safe."

"I had some antique jewelry stolen before Connor ever came to town, and we even knew the most probable suspect. Did you ever catch her? No. So here you are, profiling Connor because he's an easy solution."

Connor glanced between them. "Feel free to get a warrant and search my cabin behind Paul's house. Or my truck, which will be at Red's garage until probably forever. I have nothing to hide."

Todd's eyes narrowed on him. "And yet I have a witness. Where were you last night?"

"This is ridiculous, Todd. Why would he throw away his freedom for—"

"I'm talking to him, Keeley. Not you."

"There's no need to be rude to her," Connor said mildly. "I spent the entire day painting one of Paul's cabins. Keeley came by at around six to have supper with her dad, and I went for a walk out into the country and back. Then I had supper by myself and read for a few hours before turning in."

"And during that walk, you seemed mighty interested in the florist shop. Why is that?"

Keeley snorted. "I can't believe this. So you think he stole *daisies*?"

"They also carry pricey gift items. Some original oil paintings by local artists. Signed and numbered figurines. Any of which could be sold on eBay…by someone who wants to make some easy money." Todd leveled his gaze at Connor. "And we all know someone who is in a bit of a financial fix, given where he's been the past five years. And given that his set of wheels is sitting at Red's."

"I've never even been on eBay. I would have no idea how to turn stolen items into cash. And I'd have no use for anything those stores might carry. As for the florist, I'm still a little stiff and sore after pulling Kyle from the river and I happened to stop there to catch my breath. I remember thinking Keeley might like some of those flowers, and then I walked on."

"So that's what your so-called witness saw? A man glancing in a window? Give me a break." Keeley reined in her growing anger. "But it seemed like a simple answer to blame a man who has served time yet was *proven* innocent of any crimes, so here you are."

Todd's glare wavered. "It's my job to find the perpetrator."

"Then do it. Find the real person who did it," she snapped. She looked up at Connor. "Have you even been in those stores? Ever?"

She saw a glimmer of amusement in his eyes as he shook his head.

"So, Todd—did you find his fingerprints in any of those places? Connor would be in that computer fingerprint system you law-enforcement people use, so it would be easy enough to check. APHID?"

Todd choked back what might have been a laugh. "AFIS."

"Well?"

"No…no clear prints. But with hundreds of customers coming and going, it would be hard to tell." He rested a hand on the doorknob then turned back. "Keeley may be your big defender now, but she likes taking on hard-luck cases. Don't think I won't be watching you, Rafferty. We may be a small town, but we never, ever, give up until justice is served."

The job he hadn't even wanted was proving to be the one way he'd be able to finance the trip to reach his son, and for that Connor was grateful. If everything worked out, he would have enough money for the repairs on his truck just about the time the work was done, and then he could be on his way.

And working with Keeley had its own rewards—seeing the sparkle in her eyes and hearing her silvery laugh as the customers poured in the door made every hour brighter.

He couldn't help but chuckle every time he thought about her defending him from the deputy like an angry mama bear defending her cubs, and he wasn't even family.

But while she surprised and delighted him in some new way every day, the customers were another story.

Pushing, jostling around a display of 75-percent-off ornaments, a gaggle of hefty women wearing sequined casino ball caps managed to knock over a tall spinner rack filled with antique-style greeting cards just before noon.

Later, a man with a cunning glint in his eyes and a superior attitude unsuccessfully tried to haggle with Keeley on the price of a collector figurine, and two women argued between themselves over the right to buy an antique doll.

It was nearly six o'clock now and the crowds out on the sidewalk were finally thinning. Most of them seemed to be heading toward the festivities at the fairgrounds on the edge of town, several blocks away.

Even from here, Connor could hear the raucous sounds of the carnival rides and an indie rock band, and whenever the front door opened the aromas of popcorn, pizza and mini doughnuts wafted in.

While Keeley assisted a customer dithering over some sort of lace thing, Connor finished ringing up a sale and counted four more customers waiting in line at the register.

At a commotion coming from the front door, he looked up to see a harried mother tugging an overtired, whining toddler with a dripping ice-cream cone. Before Connor could remind her about the No Food, No Drinks sign on the door, the boy dropped his ice cream on the floor and screamed until his mom cast an apologetic glance toward Keeley and reluctantly dragged him back outside.

Connor called Bobby to the front for cleanup before helping the next customer in line.

The boy trudged out a few minutes later with paper towels, a plastic bag and a damp mop, his head bowed.

As soon as Connor finished with the last customer in line, he rounded the front counter to join him. "Need any help?"

Bobby shook his head as he dropped a wad of paper towels in the bag then began mopping. He'd been subdued the past two days, with little to say, and had refused to talk about what was bothering him.

Connor hoped he hadn't been bullied at school or on the street, but after seeing how the two arrogant girls had shunned him here at the store, it was a definite possibility.

"After we close, what would you say to asking Keeley if she might want to go to the fairgrounds? Would you like to go on some rides? Maybe get some pizza?"

Bobby silently shot a sideways glance at him and shook his head, the sad expression in his eyes reflecting none of the anticipation Connor had expected.

"What kid doesn't like pizza?" Connor teased, hoping for a smile.

Bobby shrugged as he grabbed his bucket and headed back to the storeroom. From across the store, Keeley eyed him with concern and then caught Connor's eye and tipped her head toward the back of the store.

Connor followed Bobby and watched as he carefully put away the mop and tossed the towels in the trash, then picked up a duster and started for the front of the store. "Wait, Bobby. Is something wrong?"

The boy shook his head, staring at the floor.

"Are the kids at school bothering you?"

Another silent shake of his head.

"Is everything all right at home?"

He hesitated then gave a single nod.

"You do know that Keeley cares about you, right? I'm new around here, so I understand if you don't want to talk to me. But if you're in some kind of trouble she would really try to help you. If nothing else, it can really help to just talk things over."

"No," Bobby blurted. He darted a glance at Connor, his eyes wide with fear. Then he shuffled toward the front of the store. "I gotta work now."

An hour later the shelves had been restocked and neatened, Bobby had gone home and Keeley had finished up her bookkeeping.

"I've been looking forward to this weekend and I'm

thankful that business has been good," she said with a laugh. "But now I am so ready to go home."

Connor went to the storeroom to grab his jacket. "Did Bobby ever talk to you?"

"Nope. I saw him cuddling the cat a while ago, his head down on Rag's fur. He just seems so very sad." She frowned. "I tried to talk to him before he left, but he grabbed his backpack and took off."

"He's lucky to have someone like you in his corner." Connor thought back to his own troubled teen years. "Not every kid has that."

"I just hope everything is all right at home. I might stop over there later with some excuse or another, just to make sure." She glanced at the clock. "Dad has lots of leftovers for tonight, so I'm not cooking. Want to join me up at the fairgrounds for a bite to eat?"

"That sounds better than my own plans—a long walk and leftover chili."

She pulled on her jacket, locked the doors behind them and they strolled toward the fairgrounds amid a crowd of people filling the street.

"There are two food tents run by the local churches. The Community Church is known for their hot roast beef sandwiches and fried chicken. Faith Church is known for pulled pork sandwiches, pizza and their huge hamburgers." She looked up at him and grinned. "Or if you prefer carnival food, there'll be corn dogs, deep-fried Wisconsin cheese curds, deep-fried pickles, deep-fried Snickers and cotton candy. Which I think represent all of the most important food groups. Sort of."

The sun hovered on the horizon, tinting the scattered clouds rose and blue. In the soft light of approaching dusk, Keeley's pale hair gleamed and her skin took on a soft, luminous glow. She was truly so beautiful that she took his breath away.

"So what's wrong with the local guys that none of them have nabbed you by now?"

"I haven't a clue." She laughed and looped her arm through his. "Though since it seems to be a pretty universal situation, it must be my fault. I date someone for a while. Then eventually we drift apart and end up as friends."

"*Your* fault?" The warmth of her arm in his shot straight to his chest, making him want to deck the guys who had made her doubt herself. Making him want to thank them for being so blind.

He looked down at her in wonder. "It can't have been anything to do with you. You're smart, kind, and you have the biggest heart of anyone I've ever met. You fiercely defend your friends. Oh, and you're beautiful, but it's the other stuff that matters."

"I'm not sure that's all true, but thanks." She laughed. "Then maybe it's just that I haven't met the right person yet."

Maybe you have, his inner voice whispered.

Though he had so little to offer anyone like her, he would never say that aloud.

Across the street, past the entrance of the fairgrounds, colorful carnival lights swirled and spun on the rides spinning up into the night sky. The laughter and shrieks of the kids competed with the cacophony of the midway music and the carnies shouting invitations to a row of tents offering games no one could win.

In stark contrast, a lone, familiar figure stood in the shadows outside the gate, hunched over, his arms wrapped around his waist as if someone had just landed a blow. A moment later he dropped to his knees then sagged against the trunk of a tree.

"Oh, my," Keeley breathed as she started to run. "Is he hurt? Please—get ready to call 9-1-1."

Connor followed, scanning the darkness for possible threats. His stomach clenched at the thought of someone taunting or physically harming Bobby just because he was big, and harmless, and too trusting. A child with special needs who would never quite fit in.

Life was unfair—Connor had learned that lesson himself.

And if he found out someone had hit Bobby, that person would be learning a lesson, too—but with an arrest, not a bully's fist.

Chapter Sixteen

"Hey, Bobby," Keeley murmured as she knelt next to him and rested a hand on his shoulder. "Are you okay?"

He jerked away and pressed his face against the tree.

"I need to know what happened, honey, and I'm not leaving until I do. Did someone hurt you?"

Connor hunkered down next to them. "If that happened, you don't need to be afraid. Both of us can help. And Keeley has good friends in the sheriff's department, so—"

"No! L-leave me alone." His voice broke on a sob. "Just go away."

"Friends can't do that, Bobby." Keeley rubbed his back. "I can't just leave you here if something is wrong."

He didn't answer.

"Is your aunt Bess home? Do you want me to call her?"

He shook his head violently.

"Do you want us to take you home?"

"N-no. S-she isn't there anyway."

Keeley looked up as several cars drove past and turned into the lane leading to the fairground parking lot. Some of the deputies might well be patrolling the fairgrounds, and if one of them came by, she would have Connor flag him down. "You need to tell me, so I'll ask you again. Did anyone hurt you?"

He lifted his tearstained face and shook his head, but his gaze darted away and she knew he was lying.

"Okay…for now. Connor and I were just heading over here for something to eat. Want to join us? I hear the pizza and the hot roast beef sandwiches are really good this year. And the all-you-can-eat chicken is always amazing."

He started to shake his head again but then his stomach rumbled and she slid her arm around his shoulders to give him a hug. "I think you'd better come with us and have some supper. My treat."

They walked through the crowds in the midway to the food tents, where long lines of people were waiting to be served. "This is obviously a popular choice. So what's your favorite—crispy fried chicken, pizza or the hot roast beef?"

"Chicken," Bobby murmured with such reverence that both Connor and Keeley chuckled.

"While you guys are waiting, I need to make a quick phone call. I'll be back in a moment." Keeley slipped out of line and headed for a quiet area beyond the petting zoo and the Aspen Creek Quilters' booth with its colorful display of quilts.

She dialed the home phone number at Bess's place and let it ring until the answering machine kicked in. She left a message about Bobby eating supper with her at the fairgrounds and promised he'd be home by ten.

But where was she?

Uneasy now, Keeley Googled the number of the Pine Cone Tap by Bess's house. A surly bartender answered on the sixth ring, the noise of a rowdy crowd and a jukebox blaring in the background making it nearly impossible to hear him.

"She didn't bother to show up tonight, so she's fired.

But even if she was here, no one takes personal calls here. Not *ever.*" He slammed down the receiver.

Troubled, Keeley considered the possibilities as she walked back to the Community Church food tent and joined Connor and Bobby just as they were at the front of the line ordering.

Olivia looked up at them and smiled. "Hey, Bobby, Keeley. Nice to see you." Her gaze veered over to Connor. "This must be your new employee?"

"Connor, this is Olivia—one of my book-club friends. Connor will be working at the shop for a few more weeks."

"Good. So what will you have? The chicken is excellent tonight, if you want to give it a try."

Keeley checked with Bobby and Connor, then placed her order with theirs, insisting on paying the tab when Connor reached for his wallet. "Consider this employee appreciation night. On me," she said lightly. Once they'd settled at a table with their heaping platters of food, she watched Bobby attack his meal as if he were starving.

When he finally slowed down, she sipped her coffee and chose her words carefully. "This all looks wonderful, doesn't it? By the way, I called your aunt to let her know you were eating with us, so she wouldn't worry."

Bobby froze, an extra-crispy chicken leg halfway to his mouth.

"She wasn't home, though," Keeley added. "So I hope this is okay with her. Any idea where she is?"

Bobby shifted uneasily. "Working. She said she would be working at the bar tonight."

"Ah. Of course. Does she still work at the Pine Cone?"

He nodded. "Every night but Monday and Tuesday."

So why hadn't she shown up to work? Then again, the woman could have been asleep when Keeley called. In the bathtub. Or just ignoring landline calls as so many people did to avoid irritating robocalls from companies selling something.

But with a teenage boy who wasn't home, how could anyone not answer the phone?

Since meeting Bobby several years ago, he'd always been a sweet, honest and forthright teen—never late for work, never dishonest with her. As far as she could tell.

Yet in the space of a few days, his lies and half-truths were stacking up like cord wood for the winter and his tension was palpable.

So what on earth was wrong?

After Bobby finished his chicken, Keeley led the way to the petting zoo, where she and Connor sat on a park bench watching Bobby pet the baby goats, lambs and calves. Her heart warmed when he moved on to the enclosure filled with chicks and ducklings, a huge smile on his face as he asked the supervisor a barrage of questions.

"He seems so enthralled that I wonder if he's ever been to a real zoo," she murmured to Connor. "It's so sad, really. I do think his aunt loves him, but he has missed out on so many of the things other kids take for granted."

"You've done a lot for him, though." Connor glanced down at her, frank admiration and another, deeper emotion in his eyes. "Sounds like he's needed a good influence in his life."

She bit her lip. "I try, but it's just not enough."

"He's been blessed to have you." Connor watched Bobby move on to study the reptiles contained in a long row of glass aquariums. "I remember hearing a sermon as a kid. Something about how God uses people around us to provide help, emotional support and comfort in answer to our prayers. That's what you do for Bobby."

Surprised, she glanced at him. "I didn't realize that you're a believer."

"That's how I was raised, but once I went to college I got cocky. Figured I was my own man and didn't need help from my dad, other people or even the Lord above." A corner of his mouth lifted in a faint, rueful smile. "It was one of many reasons my dad and I fought. Now that I'm older, I realize he was right."

"You're sure welcome to come to church with me, if you'd like."

"I'll think about it." Connor hooked one ankle across his opposite thigh and leaned back. "I sorta had a falling-out with God, but then had five long years to dwell on it."

"That's a long time to hold a grudge. Did it help? Being angry, that is."

"It's kind of hard to let go when you stay behind bars year after year." He slid a glance at her then lifted his gaze to the darkening sky, where thin ribbons of gold and red trailed along the horizon. "But I'm working on it."

"A lot of people think that if God is so all-powerful, then he should keep us from harm and fix everything that goes wrong." She tipped her head and looked at him. "I figure He gave us free will, so we make our own mistakes, might be at the wrong place at the wrong time, or can be at the mercy of those who choose evil over good. But God doesn't make the bad things happen."

Bobby came over to stand beside them.

"Can we go to the midway and see the rides?"

"Better than that. I think you should go on them, don't you?" Keeley reached into her pocket and pulled out a long strip of tickets. "I bought these while you guys were standing in line at the food tent. I hope you can use them up, because I hate heights and those rides give me a bad case of vertigo."

Bobby had been tearful when they'd found him by the fairground entrance and still subdued while eating supper, but now he broke into a smile from ear to ear. "Really? All of them?"

She handed them over. "Have at it, kid. I think there's enough for every ride here. You deserve a good time. We'll be on the bench by the Ferris wheel when you're ready to leave."

During their long wait, Connor had draped his arm around her shoulders and she'd leaned against him to savor his warmth against the chilly night air. It felt so right, sitting there with him…even if several passersby had looked at them and raised an eyebrow as they strolled past.

"I want to apologize for Todd," she said after a long pause. "He grew up in town and it seems like he's still trying to prove something to everyone. That's all I can figure out, anyway."

Connor looked down at her with frank admiration. "He probably has a crush on you."

"Well, if he does he'd better watch out. His fiancée is a tough cookie and she'll lay into him good if she detects a wandering eye." Keeley snorted. "They're a good match, because he's the most bullheaded man I ever met. I promise you I won't let him railroad you. And if it comes to that, I'll have my lawyer take care of it."

He chuckled. "I don't need one with you around. Have you ever thought about law school?"

"For about five minutes in high school, until I job-shadowed someone."

They settled into companionable silence, watching Bobby move from one ride to another.

But an hour later Bobby was on the roller coaster for the third time and Keeley was long past ready to go home. Still, seeing the teen screaming with delight on one ride after another had made her day. He'd even found a buddy—

a boy with thick glasses whom he seemed to know from school.

"You must be tired," Keeley said, raising her voice over the noise of the midway. "You don't have to wait here with me if you just want to go home."

Connor gave her shoulders a quick squeeze. "I'll stick around. Since you're taking Bobby home, I'd like to come along. You mentioned his house is behind some run-down bar, so that can't be very safe on a Friday night."

Keeley had taken Bobby home after work many times and had nearly declined Connor's offer to come along.

Now, looking at Bess's dark, forbidding shack of a house, she was glad he was with her. Honky-tonk music blasting from the Pine Cone Tap was so loud she could feel the vibration beneath her feet. A trio of men lounged against the back door and stared at her, the smell of their cigarettes wafting through the windows of her SUV.

Rolling up the windows, she put it in Park and looked over her shoulder. "Where do you think your aunt is, Bobby?"

"Working," he mumbled, not meeting her eyes.

"Where?"

He tipped his head toward the bar. "She always works there."

"I called your house and the bar before we had supper, to let her know you were with me. She didn't answer at home and a guy at the bar said she didn't show up." Keeley dredged up her sternest look. "Is there something you aren't telling me?"

Clutching the backpack he held on his lap, he squirmed in his seat. "No."

"Bobby?"

He dropped his gaze to his backpack. "She maybe doesn't feel good."

"Like the flu? A bad cold? Should I go in and check on her?"

He shook his head as he opened his door. "Thanks for everything. I gotta go."

He hurried to the front door of the house, bowed under the weight of his backpack and let himself in.

Keeley sighed. "Doesn't that woman ever lock her doors?"

She waited for the lights to blaze on inside the house, but it remained eerily dark. "If I go knock on the door this late at night, it might scare Bess half to death. But if I don't, I won't sleep for thinking about her."

Connor nodded. "I imagine she's had her share of drunks from the bar pounding on her door. Try calling her again."

"Good idea." Keeley pulled out her cell phone, found Bess's number and put the cell on speakerphone.

But once again the call landed at the answering machine.

Connor frowned. "Does she have a landline or a cell?"

"Landline."

"So even if her power is out, her phone should ring. Why didn't Bobby pick up your call?" He stepped out of the vehicle and strode up the dark sidewalk, then knocked loudly on the door. "Bobby? It's me—Connor. Are you all right?"

Keeley joined him and peered in the window next to the door, then tapped the flashlight app on her smartphone. "This is so strange. At least Bobby should be here."

The door creaked open a couple of inches. "What do you want?" Bess's voice quavered. "Just go away."

"It's Keeley, Bess. We just dropped Bobby off a few

minutes ago, but the lights never came on and no one answered the phone. Is everything all right?"

"Yes. Now please go."

She started to push the door shut but Keeley moved her foot to block it, then lifted the flashlight beam to waist level, enough to weakly illuminate the older woman's face.

Heavy bruising darkened one eye and there was a dark bruise on the opposite cheekbone.

Keeley gasped. "What on earth happened to you?"

"Nothing—nothing at all. I just tripped on a rug and fell. Please—just go. I'm not feeling well and I'm trying to sleep." But the urgency in her voice and her darting gaze told a different story.

"Is there someone in there with you who did this?" Connor whispered. "We can help. Or we can call 9-1-1."

"No. No, of course not," she snapped. "I was clumsy. I fell. End of story. I want to go back to bed, so don't you dare call anyone. Hear? There's no need."

"Then would you let us come inside for a minute just to be sure everything's okay? I'm worried about you, Bess," Keeley said quietly.

"Don't be," she pleaded. "Look, my husband is asleep on the sofa and he's had a long day. If you wake him up he won't be happy. He'll never get back to sleep tonight."

Startled, Keeley stared at her. "Your husband?"

"Please, just leave us alone."

"All right, then," Keeley said quietly. "But you have my number and I'll always be willing to help you any way I can. Okay?"

When Bess pushed the door shut in her face, Keeley stared at it for a moment, her heart sinking.

Maybe Bess had been truthful… It was *possible* that she'd fallen.

But it wasn't likely.

And she either didn't want help and would be embarrassed if a deputy stopped by—or she was afraid to ask. But if Keeley called the sheriff's office and law enforcement showed up, would the poor woman suffer even greater consequences? And what about Bobby? Or the mysterious husband?

Keeley started to pray.

Chapter Seventeen

Keeley parked in front of Dad's house, her thoughts troubled. "That sure was strange, with those creepy-looking guys loitering outside the bar and staring at us, and the way Bess was acting."

"Seems like a rough area."

"During the day it's just a sad, run-down part of town with litter and junker cars everywhere. At night, with the rough kind of people who hang around that bar, it's scary. Thanks so much for coming along."

"My pleasure."

"I just wish Bobby didn't have to live there. What kind of environment is that for raising a teenage boy?"

"He's a good kid, so someone must be trying to raise him right." Connor flashed a smile in the darkness. "I suspect you've had a big part in it."

"I just wish I could do more." She stared out into the darkness. "And despite what Bess said, I'm still wondering if I should call the sheriff's office tonight for a welfare check. She didn't look good at all."

Connor opened his car door partway but made no move to get out. "True, but it sounds like she wouldn't thank you for it. And she'll likely tell a deputy the same thing she told you—that she fell."

"Those bruises were nasty, and I don't believe her story about falling." Keeley shuddered. "Though I've smelled alcohol on her breath many times before, so I suppose it's possible. Still, what if someone is in her house, terrorizing her?"

"I'd guess she would've seemed far more nervous or scared, but I'm no expert. Anyway, it's pretty clear that she has little money and no worldly goods worth stealing. Why bother with her house when there are McMansions a few blocks away?"

"Unless the stranger was a Hannibal Lecter type," Keeley shot back darkly. "And what was that about a husband? I've never seen any sign of one in all the times I've picked Bobby up or dropped him off, and he's never said a word about having an uncle here in town. He was agitated today, though. So what's going on?"

"Maybe Bess and her husband were separated long ago and he came back. Or maybe he travels a lot." Connor shrugged. "Or she could have a new boyfriend staying over."

"Either way, I don't think I'll sleep tonight unless I call the sheriff's office," Keeley said on a long sigh. "If a deputy shows up at Bess's door, I just hope she doesn't blame it on Bobby, thinking he'd said something to us. It would be much harder to help him if he wasn't allowed to work at the store."

Connor studied her for a moment with a hint of a smile. "You are one amazing woman," he said after a long pause. "If I was in trouble I'd definitely want you in my corner."

The dark interior of her SUV suddenly seemed smaller, more intimate, and she found herself transfixed by the long black lashes shading his silvery blue eyes. The lean, strong lines of his face. And his mouth…

Oh, my.

The more time she spent with him, the more compelling he was, and the more dangerous to her fragile heart.

She'd never felt this kind of connection with someone, had never found her wayward thoughts drifting toward wedding bells and babies and forever-afters. Not one man in her life had ever come close.

She'd known him such a short time that those thoughts were foolish. And yet—she'd seen how caring and concerned he was with Bobby, how kind he was with her irascible father. How he'd risked his life in the river for a boy he barely knew.

Just once, before he walked out of her life, she hoped for a single kiss. A long, mind-blowing kiss that she could hold in her heart and remember forever.

She jerked herself back to reality. "Uh, thanks for letting me ramble on for so long. It really helped just having someone listen."

Connor stepped out of the vehicle and braced an arm on the roof. "Anytime. You're a wonderful person, Keeley. Don't ever doubt it," he murmured softly. "Keep safe. And sleep well."

And with that, he was gone.

Hoping for even larger crowds at the store on Saturday, Keeley had asked Connor to come to the store instead of painting another cabin.

But as he entered the store through the back door, she met him with a worried frown. "I did call the sheriff's office last night," she murmured. "I kept seeing Bess's bruises and I was worried about her."

The bells over the front door of the shop jangled. She

glanced over her shoulder toward the front of the store then lowered her voice. "And then I called the sheriff's office again this morning to ask about her, but the receptionist wouldn't tell me anything because of 'privacy issues.' And now Bobby is late for work."

"Yoo-hoo," a woman's voice trilled. "Is anyone here? I'd like to buy the children's rocker in the front window."

Connor lowered his voice. "Do you want me to go check on him?"

She glanced at the clock above the workbench and tossed her car keys to him. "If he isn't here in a half hour, yes. You could just say you've come to give him a ride to work."

The bells over the front door jangled again and he heard more footsteps coming in.

"In the meantime, you cover the cash register and I'll help the customers. Okay?"

He nodded and followed her into the store, where three customers were wandering through the aisles, looking at the displays.

One of them, a woman with tight gray curls and a shape like a chest of drawers, eyed him with dawning recognition and scurried over to intercept him as he headed for the front counter.

"Why, you're the young man who saved the Gordon boy during the flood. Connor something. Connor..." She turned. "Marge! Remember that story about the flood here in town? This is the hero who saved the senator's boy!"

Her companion, who was as spindly and tall as the first woman was round, came over with a smile and offered her hand. "It isn't often my sister and I get to meet someone like you. The article in our Chicago paper said you actually risked your life for that boy."

He shifted uncomfortably, at a loss for words, and thought

longingly of the pails of paint back at the cabin. There it was quiet and peaceful, with just the soft rustle of the breezes through the pines.

Here in town, someone stopped him in the street or came up to him in the store every now and then, and he never knew what to say. He hadn't been heroic at all. He'd automatically reacted to the situation, without a thought.

The people who had heard about his prison experience, thanks to someone named Millie or the newspaper article, and rudely asked questions about that, were a little harder to take.

"Connor," Keeley called from across the store. "Could you see if that gentleman could use some help?"

She was giving him a knowing look and sending a lifeline, which he gladly took. "Thanks, ladies." He nodded at them and headed for the man studying the display case of antique jewelry with a baffled expression.

He looked up, his forehead furrowed. "I was here yesterday midafternoon, and I'm very interested in several garnet pieces—an ornate bracelet of Bohemian garnets, earrings and a heavy gold ring. From the 1800s, the tags said. But they aren't here. Were they sold?"

"I wasn't here yesterday. Keeley?"

"I heard." She joined them at the display case. "Are you sure they aren't there? I would remember selling them, because I actually wished I could afford to keep them, as they were so beautiful. They came from the estate of a woman I admired very much."

She unlocked and opened the sliding doors at the back of the case and pulled out one tray after another until she'd searched each one, then sank back on her heels. "This is unbelievable. The case is always locked. I was the only one working here yesterday, so I had the only key with me all day."

The door bells jangled again, but she didn't look up. "It isn't like I ever have diamonds here, but that jewelry was the most expensive I've carried, and the three pieces easily totaled at least two grand. Probably more, if I'd listed them on an eBay auction."

The customer's face fell as he turned to leave. "They would have been a perfect gift for my wife. But thanks anyway."

"Another theft, I take it?"

At the all-too-familiar voice, Connor stepped aside as the deputy came forward to lean a beefy arm on the glass case.

"I guess so," Keeley said with a sad smile. "I can't believe it. I'm always so careful."

"The front and back doors were locked when you came in this morning?"

"Locked tight. The only main-floor window that can be opened is in the back, and it was locked, as well. I know, because I opened it a tad when I got here."

"So it was either an inside job or a customer."

"Look, Todd. I—"

"Okay, okay." Todd held up both hands to her, palms out. "Far be it from me to suggest an inside job. Because you *absolutely* know that couldn't be true."

His gaze slid over to Connor and held. "Quite an operation you have going for yourself, buddy. But you are going to slip up and you are going to get caught. Red-handed. And then I promise that there won't be any early releases coming your way."

Keeley crossed her arms across her chest. "Barring your instant assumption, do you have any leads at all? Since this is the fifth theft in town that I know about, surely you must have found *something*."

Todd bristled. "I've stopped by every store to warn the

owners. I've alerted the consignment stores and pawnshops throughout the county. And if a store doesn't have surveillance cameras, I'm recommending they be installed."

"Fingerprints?"

"I've tried, but nothing has turned up. So either this is someone who has never been arrested and fingerprinted, or he's been wearing gloves." Todd waved everyone away from the jewelry case. "Don't touch anything. I'll go get my fingerprint kit and hope that this time I can find a match."

By the time Todd finished lifting prints from the jewelry case and the shelf where the pieces had been displayed, a small crowd of tourists and their children had gathered to gawk over his shoulder.

"That's about it," he said, standing to gather his supplies. "You folks can go on about your business."

"I need to talk to you," Keeley said quietly. "Could you come to the back room with me?"

"Are you gonna scold me again? If so, I think I just got an emergency call out to someplace else."

"No scolding." Leaving Connor to watch the store, she led the way to the back room away from the customers. "Last night we took Bobby home after an evening at the park, and I've been worried ever since."

Todd frowned. "We? As in you and Rafferty?"

"I shouldn't have to discuss my personal life, Todd. But, yes—with Connor Rafferty. I asked Bobby if he'd like to join me for supper, and I gave him a fistful of tickets so he could go on the rides. But when we took him home, his aunt Bess was secretive and she had some pretty big bruises. And now Bobby is two hours late for work and he's *never* late. I'm worried about them both."

Todd hitched a shoulder, clearly uncomfortable. "I can't really talk to you about it."

Keeley paced to the far end of the room then returned and threw her hands in the air. "I hit this roadblock every time. Hospital. School. Social workers. I understand the privacy laws. I really do. But I'm trying to help that poor kid, and no one makes it easier. As far as I can tell, no one is interceding on his behalf. I honestly wish I had custody of him so he'd have a better life."

Todd pursed his lips and seemed to carefully think through his response. "What if someone had a guardian—or parent—who hypothetically had something like, say...serious diabetes and heart disease. Who is maybe known for low blood sugars—where she's sometimes nearly comatose and has to go off to the hospital. Or ends up there with angina."

"I already knew Bess is diabetic, with heart disease," Keeley said quietly. "I didn't realize she was that bad."

"I'm only talking hypothetically, remember," Todd admonished her. "And only because I know how much you've been trying to help Bobby."

"So a deputy did visit her last night?" Keeley prompted.

"On a drive-by security check, around two in the morning. He thought it strange that she was sitting on her front steps in the dark, so he went up to check."

"Oh, no," Keeley breathed.

"At first he thought she was drunk, because her voice was slurred and she seemed really foggy. But then he saw her Medical Alert bracelet and he called the EMTs. Apparently she'd really bottomed out, so they took her to the ER and got her blood sugar back up."

"But she had bruises before then. I saw them. Can't you do something about it?"

"Not if she denies being assaulted and there aren't any

witnesses. The deputy asked her, and she said she'd fallen on the stairs yesterday."

But when Todd wouldn't quite meet her eyes, Keeley knew he didn't believe that story, either. "Was anyone else in the house last night? She wouldn't let us in yesterday evening. She said something about her husband being asleep inside."

"In all the calls I've had to that house, I've rarely seen any sign of Rafe. He doesn't often show up in town, but apparently he is staying at her house now."

"That worries me. A lot."

"I would definitely stay away from there if I were you. It was quiet on my shift yesterday, so I went through the records clear back to our precomputer days. His name brought up a list of old charges as long as your arm—most for domestic abuse. He's had several convictions and served time in prison."

Keeley shuddered. "It's a shame he isn't still there. Poor Bess."

Todd sighed heavily. "But he won't be going back unless she tells the truth. If he was brought to court, she could deny everything and the case would be tossed."

"Maybe she's afraid he'll kill her in revenge if it comes to that."

Todd frowned. "Speaking of retaliation, the bartender at the Pine Cone called us. Rafe was there at closing time, and you wouldn't want to hear the choice names he's been calling you because you showed up at the house yesterday and 'interfered' in his life."

"All I did was talk to Bess," Keeley protested.

"He's a violent man, Keeley. No one you want to mess with—not in any way."

"But Bobby—"

"Is not your responsibility. His social worker is working

on finding a temporary foster-care placement, and we'll be patrolling the area around that house very carefully."

"You think you can watch Rafe every minute in the meantime? I doubt it."

"Don't worry about him. He ended up serving only part of his last sentence thanks to a lenient judge. But one false step—that we can prove—and he'll be back behind bars to finish his time, plus whatever new convictions he racks up." He glanced at his watch. "I've got to leave. Just promise me that you'll stay clear of this whole situation."

She offered only a vague nod, but after Todd left through the back door of the shop, she bowed her head in silent prayer.

Please, Lord, protect Bobby and his aunt, and keep them safe. And guide me to do whatever it takes to help them. In Jesus's name, I pray.

Whatever Todd thought, she knew that random drive-bys by a deputy would not prevent Rafe from another episode of domestic abuse, and someday, Bess and Bobby might not survive.

Chapter Eighteen

Keeley settled into her usual pew and savored the comforting scents of burning candles and the lemon-oil polish that gave the old oak pews a rich golden glow. This morning—Praise the Lord—the sun was shining, casting jewel-toned splashes of color across the sanctuary.

She glanced around. All of the regular members were here, as usual, as well as a scattering of tourists who were probably in town for the Antique Walk events.

She couldn't see Bobby anywhere, and her heart fell.

The church was midway between her apartment over the store and Bess's house, so each of them walked to the service on Sunday mornings and he usually sat beside her. He hadn't shown up at the store yesterday, either. Had his uncle Rafe made him stay home? Was he all right?

A flutter of murmurs rippled through the congregation and, a split second later, a little shiver of awareness coursed through her. From the corner of her eye she saw a tall man in a black oxford shirt and Levi's pause at the end of her pew. "Do you mind?"

"Connor! Of course I don't mind. If I'd known you were coming I would have waited for you outside."

"Apparently your dad didn't want to come. I went up to the house and asked him, though."

"I'm afraid that will never happen," she whispered back. "He's rarely set foot in a church since Mom died, but I never quit hoping."

She tipped her head toward the front of the church, where a towering stained-glass window depicted Jesus as a shepherd surrounded by a flock of sheep. "Isn't that beautiful? The church was built in 1879 and the stained-glass windows are all original. When I was little, I spent most of my time here just looking at the pretty windows."

A hush fell over the congregation as the organist began a hauntingly beautiful rendition of "Beautiful Savior" followed by a soloist singing "Amazing Grace."

During those incredible soaring notes Keeley felt her cares float away, and she melted bonelessly against the pew, her contentment complete...except for her ever-present worries about Bobby, and the knowledge that her dad remained too hard-hearted to join her here.

How could he not want to be surrounded by this place of faith, where he'd been baptized, confirmed and married, with so many people he'd known all his life?

His long-standing bitterness only poisoned him further, but after all these years there seemed to be no hope that he'd ever change.

She looped her arm through Connor's as they walked back to her dad's home after the service. "Thanks so much for coming."

"I'm glad I went." He glanced down at her. "Like I said, it's been a long time. I tried a prison Bible-study class for a while, trying to find answers about my life, but maybe I just wasn't ready to listen then. But I did challenge myself to read the Bible clear through."

Surprised, she looked up at him and gave his arm a

squeeze. "Not many people accomplish that. Good for you."

He grinned. "Guess I had some years without much else to do."

"Did you discover anything surprising?"

"Some things have taken a long while to think through and I can't pretend to understand it all, not by a long shot. But I'm working on it." He glanced up at the robin's-egg-blue sky and fluffy clouds. "I was angry at God for a long while, thinking He didn't care enough to listen to my prayers. It sure seemed like He wasn't listening when my marriage failed or when I stayed in prison all that time for something I didn't do."

"And now?"

"His answers aren't always what I want to hear and don't always come right when I want them. But I realize now that He has answered me all along. I was just too stubborn to see it."

Keeley nodded. "Sometimes I'm in awe at how my prayers are answered—often in perfect ways I hadn't even considered. And I don't know how I could have survived the loss of my mom without knowing that I will be with her again, and that fills me with hope and joy. It gives me such comfort. But I still miss her, every single day."

At the next street corner they stopped to let a car pass before crossing, and he dropped an unexpected, light kiss on her temple that sent a shiver of pleasure straight through her.

"Right now, I'm thankful for ending up here," he said. "I was upset when my truck broke down on the highway, but if it hadn't, I wouldn't be here in Aspen Creek, and I wouldn't have met you."

His words wrapped around her heart. Even though he planned to leave, she would never regret the time she'd been able to spend with him…and she would never forget this moment.

"I'm thankful, too," she murmured. *More than you'll ever know.*

Connor couldn't turn down an invitation to supper with Keeley and her dad—not when she was planning to grill hamburgers out on the patio at the back of the house, practically in front of his cabin. The enticing aroma would have drawn him out of his cabin anyway. And after a long and busy Sunday afternoon working at the store, it would be nice to just sit and relax.

So Connor took over the grill, while Keeley prepared fresh mixed fruit, sautéed whole green beans and made a spinach salad with mandarin oranges and strawberries.

As he looked at the basket of warm blueberry muffins and the serving bowls she'd set out on the picnic table covered with a yellow tablecloth, it hit him all over again. *I'm free.*

At the sheer joy of it all—his freedom, a quiet Sunday evening, and this a meal under the trees on someone's patio, without cement walls or bars surrounding him—he nearly dropped to his knees in thanksgiving.

This warm family moment, with Keeley and her father and the wonderful aromas of the meal they would be eating together, made him realize something else.

He longed for this. Family. Shared meals and holidays and all the rest. It was time to reach out to his own family and try to make amends. Only by ending the years of hurt and anger could he finally feel whole. And more than that—Lord willing—Joshua *deserved* to know the rest of his family.

"You look awfully happy about hamburgers," Paul

grumbled at Connor as he settled into a chair at the table. "I'd rather have rib eye."

"Grilling outside makes everything taste better, Dad," Keeley said with a roll of her eyes. She bowed her head and led them in a simple table prayer then passed Paul a pitcher of pink lemonade. "You like this lemonade, and these are your favorite summer salads. Right?"

He eyed the spinach salad with marked distaste and passed the bowl on to Connor. "I don't eat that stuff. Never have."

"But it's your fav—" She bit back the rest of the sentence and shot a glance at Connor, mouthing the words *bad day.* "You're right, Dad. I forgot."

"Well, don't serve that again."

Connor shifted in his seat, sensing the hint of frustration beneath Keeley's carefully tactful response.

He'd already come to see that there wasn't much consistency between Paul's opinions from one day to the next, and his brief bouts of confusion were often followed by flashes of irritability. Keeley tried to calm and placate him whenever possible but it didn't always work—sometimes Paul saw through her effort and was affronted by what he claimed was condescension.

It wasn't an easy road, and Connor admired her for her grace and patience. "So, what do you want me to do this evening?"

"Goodness. You should just relax," she said, passing the colorful bowl of mixed fruit to her dad. "Go for a walk or read. There's plenty of time to take care of things around here."

"I think I'll start on the second cabin, if it's all the same to you. I have around two gallons of the paint left before I need to go after some more."

"But you don't need to do that today. Really."

"I'd rather work than sit still, and I'd rather get things done for you while I can, before I leave."

She froze for a moment. "It isn't going to be soon, though, right? You have lots of time?"

Did she feel the same as he did—already feeling a pang of regret over the day when he would continue on to Detroit? There was nothing he wanted more than to see his son, but leaving this place and this woman would bring its own kind of loss and sadness.

His feelings for Keeley had been growing with every passing day, even though he knew it couldn't last.

He came with too much baggage—a wounded heart, a vengeful ex-wife and a son who might never forgive him for being gone. By the time he sorted out his life, she undoubtedly would have found a great guy without such a checkered past.

"I won't be leaving soon. I have until Red finishes the truck and I've earned the cash to pay him. But until then, I want to keep busy." He nodded toward the cabin he'd been staying in. "That place really beats sleeping on the ground in a pup tent, so I need to earn my keep."

"Honestly, just having someone here on the property is worth a great deal. But if you really do want to start painting again, I'll help you tonight."

"Thanks. I just need to make a phone call and then we can clear the supper dishes and get started."

Connor walked over to the front porch of his cabin, hooked a boot on the front step and tapped Marsha's number in the phone book of his cell. She'd been hostile the last time, so he'd backed off and hadn't called for the past seven days.

The last thing he wanted was to spook her into making good on her threat. If she grew edgy about him coming to

Detroit, she could take off for parts unknown with Joshua in tow. How would he find her then?

She answered on the fifth ring. "It's just me, Connor," he drawled, laying on the down-home Texas charm. "How's everything going?"

She sucked in a deep breath. He heard the sound of her muffled voice, as if she'd put her hand over the phone to talk to someone in the background, and then a deeper voice rose with impatience.

She came back to the phone. "There's no point in calling. If you keep this up, I'm changing phone numbers."

Connor took a slow, calming breath. "It's been an entire week since I last called," he said mildly. "Believe me, I'm not trying to bother you. I'm happy to hear you have a new boyfriend and wish you all the best. But it's been five years since I've seen Joshua and I just want to see him again. I'd rather work this out between us than have to take legal measures. Don't you agree?"

"You want to see him—or is it that you want to take him away? I won't let that happen."

"Marsha—"

Her short laugh sounded bitter. "You plan on coming here soon? Good luck. I can promise you that we'll be long gone."

"She said what? How can she do that?" Incredulous, Keeley plopped down on the top step next to Connor and hugged her upraised knees.

"It's Marsha, so she figures she can do anything she wants. Our life together was a battleground—one-upmanship as an art form. I'm not sure if she's suddenly turned into a supermom and thinks she's protecting her child from a big bad wolf, or this is sheer vindictiveness."

"I'm so sorry, Connor. That seems so unfair."

"Either way, if she's truly planning to disappear somewhere along the East Coast, my chances of finding her there are slim to none. Apparently she's no longer concerned about waiting for the end of the school year."

"So you need to get to Detroit fast." She turned to look at him. "Still figure flying isn't the answer?"

"I did check prices and flight times, but with the hour-plus drive to the Twin Cities airport, the hours you need to be there before flights, flight time and car-rental hassles, I'd just as soon get in a vehicle here and make the ten-hour drive."

"Have you talked to Red about your truck?"

"I'll call first thing in the morning. But unless there's been some amazing progress, it won't be done soon enough. Maybe I can get a loaner car from Red."

"Red?" She laughed out loud. "Good luck with that. His loaners are wrecks and can barely top fifty with a tailwind. I had one for a week last winter and it drove me insane. The whole town avoids those junkers, believe me."

His elbows propped on his thighs, he folded his hands in defeat.

Sitting next to him on the narrow cabin steps, she could feel the tension radiating from his body and knew he must be torn up inside over this latest barrier to reaching Joshua.

She didn't want Connor to leave.

It would mark the end of her time with him here, this chance to get to know an enigmatic man who had been through so much yet had remained such a kind and thoughtful person. A man who had dominated her thoughts since the day he arrived.

But she could not stand in his way when he had so much to lose.

"I can loan you my SUV," she said quietly.

He rubbed his face with his hands and stared out at the

lawn. "But this trip could take a week, or much more, if things don't go well. I have no idea. You need your car back before then."

"You're forgetting the infamous black New Yorker. The one Dad used to leave me stranded on the store roof." She laughed softly. "I'd give you that one but doubt it would make it across the state line without needing major surgery. If it stays in this county, at least it's close to its mechanic."

"That's awfully nice of you, but—"

"No arguments. The important thing is for you to leave town and find that boy of yours in time. Now, how are you going to find him? Detroit is a big city."

"I've already called Marsha's friend Lonnie and begged for the address. All she knows is that Marsha's somewhere in the suburbs east of Detroit, but she says she has friends who might know more. She promised to call me if she hears anything. I'm also going to track down Marsha's sister and ask her."

"If you need me to do any research on the internet for you while you're driving, just call me."

"One thing—I have a feeling Marsha is going to be hostile when I appear, so I need to be prepared. Could you ask your sister if she found any names of good family-law attorneys in Detroit?"

"No problem. I'll call her right away and one of us will text you." Keeley thought for a moment. "Maybe you'd better bring a tape recorder, just to document what's said. I have one in my office."

"I can never repay you for all you've done, Keeley."

"Believe me, the pleasure has been all mine."

She studied his rugged face, already missing him. He

would need to come back here to return her SUV, but would he then need to leave right away? Would she ever again have moments like this, when she could simply enjoy his company?

"Oh—and if you do leave tomorrow, don't forget," she added, forcing a smile. "Tomorrow your sutures need to come out. You could probably stop at a walk-in clinic somewhere en route."

He chuckled. "I've lost count of how many cow and horse lacerations I sutured before leaving the ranch. I can handle a few of my own."

She ran to her car for the keys and then handed them over. "It has a full tank of gas and gets around 28 mpg, so that'll take you almost five hundred miles. I'll leave a paycheck on the seat that you can cash at the bank in the morning, on your way out of town, and I'll add a little more. If you want to leave tonight, we can figure out a way to wire you that money."

He stood slowly. He rested his hands on her shoulders, and they stared at each other silently for a long moment until he finally looked away and broke the spell.

"I don't know what to say, except…thanks. I promise you'll get your SUV back soon as I can. And I'll repay every last cent I owe you."

"I'm not worried. Just take it easy and be safe, so you get there. I'll be praying that everything goes all right."

He reached up and traced her cheek with his hand, and then he kissed her. Gently. Just a whisper of a touch, but then he kissed her again, longer this time, until she felt her toes tingle and her heart skip a beat.

But once he left for Detroit, he would be starting the next step of his new life—one that would center on his son and his life out West.

And she knew that long after this moment, when she savored the memory of that wonderful kiss, she would wonder how it could have felt so sweet, so romantic…

And still feel like a forever goodbye.

Chapter Nineteen

Connor switched his cell to speakerphone, settled it on the dashboard and listened to the ranch phone ring six then seven times.

He'd tried to call at different times of the day during his trip to Detroit, his heart racing and his palms damp, but no one ever picked up the phone and he couldn't bring himself to leave a message. He had to say this directly, or not at all.

He moved his thumb over the buttons to disconnect the call, but just then a deep, raspy voice answered.

"Dad?"

Silence. Each second seemed like an hour while he waited for his father to acknowledge him after all these years.

Finally he heard Ben Rafferty clear his throat. *"Connor?"*

Connor offered up a silent prayer for the right words that might finally heal the painful crevasse of anger that stretched out between them. "I've missed hearing your voice, Dad. I want—no, I need—to tell you that I'm sorry."

Silence.

"I'm not calling because I want anything from you. I

just want a chance to make amends. I miss you, Dad. I miss all of you."

He listened to the lengthening stretch of dead silence, surprised and relieved that Dad hadn't yet slammed down the phone.

When that didn't happen, he plowed on. "You probably didn't hear about it, but I was exonerated. Maybe you won't believe me, but Chris or Dan can look it up on the internet for you. DNA tests proved I had nothing to do with that murder. It was all a terrible mistake."

"Figured."

Connor glanced down at his cell in disbelief. If that was true, Dad certainly hadn't ever shared it. He'd never made any effort at contacting Connor. Ever. "You thought I was innocent?"

Dad mumbled something he couldn't quite hear.

"So now I'm starting my life over, but first I'm on my way to Detroit to try to get my son back—at least partial custody."

"You…" Dad's voice trembled and he cleared his throat again. "You never brought him out here."

Stunned, Connor swallowed hard at the hurt in his father's voice.

Ben had been beyond disgusted at the news of his most wayward son's shotgun marriage and subsequent divorce, and he'd never said a word about the baby. Connor had expected no softening of the old man's heart now. Was it even possible?

"You said we weren't welcome."

"Maybe…maybe it's time to put the past to rest."

Connor heard the muffled sound of him calling his other sons to the phone. Then Chris and Dan picked up receivers in other parts of the rambling ranch house.

The first awkward, tentative efforts at conversation

stumbled along for several long minutes…then dissolved in a raucous melee of voices vying to be heard. He'd expected rancor, but they actually seemed happy to hear from him. *Happy.*

Listening to them, Connor glanced heavenward. Forgiveness—could he have imagined it could feel so wonderful, like a healing balm to his soul? *Thank You, Lord. Thank You.*

When the call finally ended, with promises to keep in close touch and that he'd come to the ranch as soon as possible, Connor settled back against the seat. Any fellow drivers on the road who could see him grinning ear to ear probably thought him crazy. But that didn't matter. Not one bit.

Twenty miles down the road, he speed-dialed Keeley, his heart too full to keep his news to himself.

She was the only person on earth he could imagine sharing it with, and when she answered on the second ring he couldn't help but smile into the phone. "I can't believe what just happened, Keeley…"

She listened with rapt attention. "That's great news, Connor. I'm so thrilled for you!"

"I just hope things work out."

"Please, keep me posted on how things go in Detroit. Were you able to set up an appointment with a lawyer when you get there?"

"Eight o'clock tomorrow morning. Your sister made the contact for me—probably the reason why I was able to get something so soon."

"I wish you well. And take *lots* of notes."

Just a few minutes after they ended the call, his cell rang, and Lonnie, Marsha's friend, appeared on the caller ID screen.

He pulled off into the nearest freeway rest stop just

south of Detroit and scrambled for a pen and paper. "Did you find it? Do you have Marsha's address?"

"It wasn't easy, let me tell you. That woman picks up stakes and moves more often than anyone I ever met."

"It probably has something to do with paying rent," Connor muttered.

Lonnie gave a startled laugh. "I guess you do know her pretty well. Anyway, her last known address is 421 Harper Street, Fairbury, Michigan—which is just outside Detroit. If you don't mind, I'd rather she didn't know I was the one who helped you. She can be one vindictive woman."

"No problem. I can't thank you enough, Lonnie. I couldn't have found her without you."

The woman chuckled. "Now you can go get that sweet little boy of yours and see that he's raised right."

Her words wrapped around his heart and gave it a hard squeeze. After all this time, could it finally happen?

Connor plugged the new address into the GPS on his phone and pulled back onto the highway.

Six-hundred-fifty miles down, with seventy to go.

And with every mile he was praying that Marsha hadn't already disappeared.

Connor had dreamed of this moment for five long years. He'd tried to imagine his son's four-year-old face and how it might have changed. Wondered if Josh would even remember him—or the wrestling matches they'd played on the floor, that Joshua always won with shrieks of laughter.

The piles of books they'd read every night.

The battles with the bathtub armada of plastic boats.

When Connor arrived at the right address on Tuesday morning he took a deep breath and knocked on the door, his hand shaking.

He realized that despite the passing years, he'd been imagining Josh as a sweet little boy.

He definitely hadn't prepared himself for the much-older sullen child who now stood in the open doorway and stared at him without any sign of recognition. "My mom went to the store and Ed is sleeping." The boy started to close the door.

"Josh, don't you remember me?" Connor said softly, trying to slow his racing heart. "You were only four when I saw you last. Wow. You've changed so much. I didn't imagine you'd already be so tall."

The boy's eyes widened with fear and confusion. He pushed harder on the door. Connor stopped it with his foot, but made no move to go in.

"I'm your dad, remember? I've been gone a long time, but I've wanted to see you again more than anything in the whole world."

Josh's momentary fear turned to anger in a heartbeat. "Right. You cared so much that you killed somebody and went to jail, instead of being home like a real dad."

"I didn't do it, Josh."

"Like I should believe that." The boy's voice rose. "My mom says you're a murderer and belong in jail. She says you're crazy dangerous—and they'd never let you out. *Ever.*"

This was much harder than he'd expected. If he persisted, the boy might just get more upset. If he left, Marsha would probably grab Joshua the moment she returned and flee.

This might be Connor's only chance.

"I sent you a newspaper clipping about my release, son. Did you see it?"

Josh's lower lip trembled and he shook his head.

"Someone else killed that poor sheriff. Not me. It just

took a long time for them to finally find the mistake in the DNA testing. But because of that mistake, I missed years of watching you grow up. It makes me so sad to think about it."

"Yeah, you really cared. You never even bothered to send a stupid birthday card in all that time." The boy's voice dripped venom. "You love me, all right. Go away."

There were tears in his eyes now. Tears that gave Connor a glimmer of hope. "Didn't your mom give you the letters I wrote twice a week? The cards at birthdays and Christmas?"

Joshua wavered, glanced over his shoulder, then stood taller with renewed bravado. "I don't believe you. My mom would never steal my mail."

A man appeared in the doorway, next to Josh, with rumpled salt-and-pepper hair, a five o'clock shadow and a heavy gold 1980s chain around his neck. His eyes were bleary, but he had broad shoulders beneath an unbuttoned shirt and the beefy look of a wrestler who had gone paunchy in the midsection. Connor guessed that Marsha thought him handsome. She'd gone for his type before.

The guy surveyed Connor with narrowed eyes then rested a possessive hand on Joshua's shoulder. "What's going on here? You guys woke me up."

"Joshua?" Connor said gently. "Can you introduce us?"

"This is Ed. He and Mom are getting married." The boy dropped his gaze to the floor. He didn't sound very thrilled about it. "And this is…this is my dad. He's s'posed to be in prison."

Ouch. "Actually, I was exonerated." Connor met the other man's gaze squarely. "But Joshua doesn't quite believe it."

The other man gave a brief, tight nod. "I read about it. Marsha's been real worried about you showing up someday, so I looked it up on the internet. You got a raw deal, buddy."

Connor glanced at the room behind them. Furniture in place, framed prints on the walls, no moving boxes in sight. Had Marsha been lying about leaving town? "More than anything, I've wanted to see my son again."

"She's been stewing about that, too."

Ed seemed reasonable enough, and Connor felt another flash of hope. "I don't want her to feel that way. There's no need. I just want some time with Joshua."

"It don't matter to me. Marsha's the one you gotta deal with, and good luck with that." He hesitated and then stepped to one side. "Want to come in? The place is a mess, but you might as well sit down. She should be back soon."

Connor looked down at Joshua. "Okay with you, son?"

"Whatever." Joshua waited until Connor settled in an upholstered chair, and then he plopped down at the farthest end of the sofa.

But now his eyes were riveted on Connor as if he couldn't bear to look away.

Ed ambled into the kitchen and came back with a mug in his hand. "Coffee? I can add a little kick to it if you want."

"No, thanks."

Hitching himself onto a stool at the counter dividing the living room and kitchen, Ed took a long swig from his mug and rested a meaty arm on the counter. "I'll probably get in trouble for saying this, but I figure you gotta right to know. Those letters you sent Josh did come. But she figured they would just upset him, so far as I know, they all went in the trash. At least while I've been around. Almost a year now."

Joshua sucked in a deep breath. "She shouldn't have done that."

Ed shrugged. "Well, kid, it ain't my business. Talk to her about it."

"I understand you're moving," Connor ventured. "Anyplace fun?"

Ed's eyes gleamed. "Mississippi. That's real casino country down there along the Gulf."

Not the East Coast, then? "So you're a gambler."

"Big stakes, tall drinks, fancy women. What's not to love?"

"You must be successful at it, then." Connor glanced over at Joshua, who had slumped down into the couch. Ed's lifestyle would certainly be appealing to Marsha, but what kind of life was that going to be for his son if they were out partying all night? "What will you do with Josh?"

He shrugged. "He's old enough to be home alone and not burn the place down. Right, kid?"

Josh didn't answer.

"So…what do you play?"

"High-stakes poker, blackjack—you name it," Ed boasted. "I'm tough to beat."

Connor shuddered, thinking of the sleazy life Marsha and this man had chosen. The apartment sure didn't seem to be the home of a high roller, though. "Have you lived here long?"

Ed waved an arm dismissively. "This is a dump. Marsha's lease ends next month and then we'll be out of here. Hey—maybe you can come down and visit us. We'll show you a good time."

"Show who a good time?" Marsha walked in the door carrying a sack of groceries.

When she saw Connor her mouth fell open and she froze. The sack of groceries slid through her arms to the floor.

"What in blazes are you doing here?" Her stony gaze

veered over to Ed. "And why did you let him in? I *told* you what could happen. And yet you did it anyway, like this was some happy little tea party."

"He seems nice enough to me," Ed said mildly, taking another long swallow from his mug.

She pinned a malevolent glare on Connor. "Get out. Do you hear me? *Get out.*"

"Actually, we need to talk, but then I'll leave," Connor said quietly. "No yelling, no screaming, no name-calling. Just talk."

She glared at him, her arms folded over her chest. "There is no point. Get out of here, or I'm calling the cops."

"Your loss, if you do. I've spent the last two hours with my lawyer here in town." He flipped the man's business card on the coffee table. "Hire an attorney yourself and we can just turn this all over to the two of them and give them each twenty grand to argue. Or we can be adult about this and make it simple. If we can amicably come to a decision about shared custody and hand that over to our attorneys, it will cost each of us much, much less. Your choice."

She blinked.

"I'll take that as a vote for the economical option. Good." He nodded toward the kitchen table. "Can we sit over there and get started? Maybe you'll want to have Josh go to his room while we talk. Or Ed can take him somewhere fun for a while."

"Go to your room, kid. And shut the door." Ed lifted an arm and pointed. "*Now.* I'm going to stay with your mom."

He stood behind her chair and rested his hands on her shoulders as if protecting her from marauders.

Connor choked back a laugh. "You might as well sit down, Ed. I have no desire to pounce on your girlfriend, and this is going to take a while."

He pulled a voice-activated mini recorder from his shirt

pocket, thankful that Keeley had loaned it to him. "I want a record of what we say here, and you should record it, too. If you don't have a recorder, you can download a quick app into your smartphone and you'll be all set."

Ed whipped out his phone and got it ready.

"For starters, I've retained a family-law lawyer here in Detroit, as I said. He's very successful and he's quite a shark, but I have no interest in anything beyond ensuring that Marsha and I have equal rights in Joshua's welfare. Marsha has repeatedly stated that 'I'll never see Joshua again' and that she's 'moving away so I can never find my son again.' Obviously, that's not acceptable."

Ed frowned and looked at Marsha. "You said that? Half the time you act like you don't want the kid around."

She lifted her chin defiantly but said nothing.

"Before I was wrongly arrested, you and I had shared custody, Marsha. It was fair, and I believe it was in Joshua's best interests, though you actually had him much less because you were so...busy. That was fine with me, and it certainly freed you up for work and your social life, right?"

"We're moving south," Ed interjected. "It would hardly work to pass the kid back and forth every week. Who's gonna pay all that airfare unless you move down there, too?"

"I'm not moving south, so we'll need to split the cost fifty-fifty. It won't be cheap."

Ed scowled.

Marsha blanched.

"The courts will want to make sure each of us is a responsible parent, with steady income to support him. On my way up here I called my brothers back in Texas, and they've welcomed me back into the family ranching business." A brief image of Keeley and Aspen Creek flashed into his thoughts. "Or I may try to settle in western Wisconsin. What about you two—steady paychecks, right?"

Marsha and Ed exchanged uneasy glances.

"I'm a taxpayer," Ed said after a brief pause. "We're both solvent."

But what you want is a life of casinos, gambling and nightlife. What kind of life is that for my son? Connor cleared his throat. "Well, then, let's get down to work and figure this out."

Chapter Twenty

On Thursday afternoon Keeley took another Tylenol then slipped in the foam earplugs she'd just purchased at the drugstore and forced herself to concentrate on the bookkeeping system in her laptop.

Even with the earplugs, she could hear a hammer pounding. But it was a good thing, she reminded herself firmly. *Embrace the renovations and be glad.*

If only Connor were back in town from Detroit.

He'd been gone since early Monday morning, but though he'd called to share the news about meeting Joshua, and had been calling several times a day to report on his progress, she still missed him. A lot.

She massaged her temples, willing away the headache thudding in time to that hammer.

Now there were *three* hammers pounding in the store, none keeping time with the other, and a table saw was squealing through yet another board.

Why she'd thought these projects would be relatively unobtrusive during business hours escaped her now, but few customers had lingered today and she was counting the minutes until closing time. Still, she hadn't expected a lot of customers during the week after the Antique Walk anyway.

A blessing. This was a *blessing*, she reminded herself.

The contractor had called early this morning, saying he had a remodel cancellation, and would Keeley be interested in moving her renovation dates up on the calendar? It had taken less than a second of thought to respond in the affirmative.

So now there was a team of guys fixing the roof and fire escape. Several were downstairs taking care of the floor joists weakened by more than a century of use. Others were working on accessibility issues in the main-floor bathroom designated for customers. And after five o'clock, the old, cracked cement steps to the front and back doors would be re-poured.

Every last project on her repair and reno list would now be done just in time for a professional inspection on Friday and its presentation to the loan officer at the bank.

Rags eyed her from one of the shelves above her then leaped down onto the surface of the desk with a thud and plopped his rear on her keyboard. She stared at him in surprise. "So when did you decide to be so friendly?"

He stared at her with the arched sophistication only cats and maître d's at haute cuisine restaurants fully perfected.

"You'll really have to move, though, buddy," she said, pushing him to one side. "You aren't transparent and I can't see my screen."

He jumped to the floor, scattering invoices and receipts.

"Keeley?"

At the sound of Bobby's tremulous voice behind her, she spun around and launched from her chair to give him a quick hug. "How are you?" she exclaimed. "I missed you over the weekend."

He shuffled his feet and looked away. "I couldn't come 'cause Aunt Bess needed me. Am I fired?"

"Of course not, but I was very worried about you. I'm just glad to see you're all right." She waved a hand toward the rest of the store. "Did you see all the trucks parked out front? And the guys working inside? It's a very busy day."

He scooped up the cat and frowned at the coating of dust and bits of litter on the floor. "They made a mess."

"Yes, indeed, but it's a good mess, because they're doing things that must be done, so the bank will let me refinance this place. Would you like to do some dusting for me?"

He nodded and began dusting an old rocker, then moved on to an 1880s chest of drawers with delicate carving on the front and sides.

"How is your aunt Bess feeling now?" she asked after a few minutes. "I heard she had to go to the hospital for a while."

He shuddered. "She had to have needles and everything. But she's better now. Mostly."

"Mostly?"

He shot a troubled glance at Keeley and then dropped his gaze. "Not when Uncle Rafe is around."

"You don't like him very much?"

Bobby shook his head.

She busied herself with straightening a couple of framed prints on the wall. "Why is that?"

"He makes her cry. He's mean to her and she cries."

"Is he ever mean to you?"

Bobby's silence triggered alarms in her head and she turned slowly, tilting her head in concern. "What does he do, Bobby? Does he hurt you in any way?"

The boy looked away, his lower lip trembling.

Oh, dear Lord, she prayed silently, desperately. *Please don't let this be what I think it is.*

"No adult should ever hurt a child in any way, honey. *No* adult has that right. And if it happens, it's very important to let an adult know so it can be stopped…and can never happen again. Do you understand me?"

He kept his face averted.

"And it's important to talk about feelings with someone like a school counselor or a social worker, or a policeman or your doctor…any adult whom you trust."

He bowed his head. "U-Uncle Rafe hits people. Hard. And he yells bad words and uses his belt with a big buckle. H-he says that's the only way I'll learn, 'cause I'm stupid. And when Aunt Bess tries to stop him, he hits her, too."

It apparently wasn't the type of abuse she'd feared, but it was horrifying nonetheless. "That's terrible, Bobby. He has no right to say those things and no right to hit you or your aunt. Would you be willing to talk to a deputy, who can, um, ask Rafe to stop?"

She held her breath as he wavered then finally gave a single, small nod.

"H-he won't make Rafe mad, will he? Please d-don't make him mad at me for telling."

There were no guarantees on that score, but leaving that monster to terrify an ill, middle-aged woman and a young teen would be far worse.

"Let me make a quick phone call and then I'll help you with more dusting, okay?"

Deputy Luke Dalton, one of the older officers in town, appeared thirty minutes later with a county social worker in tow. Middle-aged, with a friendly smile and brown hair pulled up into a tipsy bun, she seemed like the perfect, non-threatening choice for Bobby and he appeared to warm up to her right away.

They visited with him privately in the back room for a good forty minutes before rejoining Keeley.

"This was perfect timing for you to call the sheriff's office about this child—I was in town for a home visit anyway, and it was canceled. I'm Debra Yates," the woman said, offering her hand. "Sorry I didn't introduce myself sooner, but Bobby seemed to be in a receptive mood and I didn't want to keep him waiting."

"I know you probably can't tell me much, but is he all right?"

Debra chuckled. "Right now he's quite content back at your worktable, because I brought him a soda and a package of Twinkies."

Keeley bit her lower lip. "Do you think it's safe for him to go back to that house?"

The social worker tapped the manila folder held in the crook of her arm. "I see that a search for foster care has been initiated, but the homes on our list are already overcrowded and we haven't been able to find him a suitable placement. Not everyone is willing to take on a teenage boy, you see."

"But is it safe for him to be at Bess's place? That's my big question. Bobby said his uncle hits him with the buckle end of a belt and tells him he is too stupid to learn any other way. Did he tell you that?"

"Yes, and so long as that man is in the house, this child should not be there. It would be a different story if the uncle were to be removed from the home and jailed for a substantial time, but at most he might be locked up for six months to a year. And then he'd be back, probably angry, and potentially more volatile than before."

"She's right, unfortunately," the deputy added. "Our judges don't view excessive corporal punishment—essentially how Rafe uses his belt—as seriously as other kinds of abuse...and emotional abuse can be hard to prove. I'll get a warrant and lock him up, but he'll soon be out on bail and right back in the community. Even if he's convicted, it won't be long enough. Unless, God forbid, he does something worse."

"So without foster-care placement, Bess's home is the only option right now...and that isn't a good idea. What about somewhere else temporarily—like my place? He's here most every afternoon anyway."

"Even though it might only mean a stay for a week or two, we need a background check and references," Debra warned. "There are a few hoops to go through first."

"No problem. I just want to make sure Bobby is safe."

The woman beamed. "He tells me that he loves being here with you, so I'll ask him what he thinks about this possible change before we go any further. If he's on board with the idea, I'll do whatever I can to expedite this. You're sure you want to take him on for a while?"

Keeley nodded decisively. "There's no doubt in my mind."

At five o'clock Keeley turned off the lights in the store and moved to the front door to lock up.

She stopped in surprise at the sight of her SUV parked in front of her store. *Connor?*

He opened the door and stepped out, and she fought the urge to break into a run to meet him, just as the hilarious Western heroine had done at the beginning of *Romancing the Stone.*

Mindful of the pedestrians on the sidewalk and Millie, who was probably keeping an eagle eye on the town from her store window, she managed to rein in her emotions until she reached him. "I'm so glad to see you! How did it go?"

"Better than I'd hoped...in most ways." He nodded toward a bench flanked with shoulder-high lilacs along the side of her building. "Can we talk?"

"Of course." Mystified, she followed him and sat on the

bench and gripped the front edge of the seat. Bad news was coming, she could feel it, and already her heart felt heavy with dread.

"It went well in Detroit," he said. "I met three times with the lawyer your sister recommended and talked with Marsha and her boyfriend Ed several times. We came to an agreement about shared custody on our own, so my lawyer was able to make an initial appointment with the court."

"That's wonderful!"

"Because of the distances involved between Texas and the Gulf, Marsha agreed to have Joshua just for the summers, but I'll have him during the entire school year. We'll alternate major holidays. But Ed isn't that fond of 'having a kid around all the time' and I wouldn't be surprised if I were to end up having Josh most of the summer, too."

She stared at him. "They're moving down to the Gulf?"

"Apparently, Ed is an insurance agent, but he's quite a gambler in his free time. He's bent on moving down there because he likes some of the casinos." Connor sighed heavily. "That lifestyle isn't the kind of example I want for Josh."

"But maybe he won't be with them very much. Otherwise, do things look good?"

"Mostly. He and Marsha have pay stubs to prove they have incomes. But before everything can be settled legally, I need to prove that I'm gainfully employed and can do my share of supporting Josh."

"What about your job here at the store?"

"I appreciate all you've done for me. But I need more income, with insurance and benefits. Unfortunately the most solid option is to head back to Texas and ranch with my brothers…at least long enough to show income and decide if that's where I belong or if I want to do something else."

A pang of sorrow lanced through her. "Texas."

He gave a short, humorless laugh. "My dad and brothers were actually happy to hear from me. Dad has a heart condition and can't do ranch work any longer, and my brothers are overwhelmed. I think they all view this as the timely return of the prodigal son."

"It's so far," Keeley whispered.

"It's my only viable choice for now. If I can't settle the custody issue right now, who knows? I may not be granted such a good opportunity later. Marsha could decide to fight back saying I'd failed to follow through this time around and couldn't be trusted in the future."

Keeley clenched her hands in her lap. "So…what's the timetable?"

"Once I get settled at the ranch, I need to go back to Detroit for a final court date and then I can bring Josh home to Texas for a few weeks before Marsha's summertime custody starts."

Her heart fell. "So you're leaving soon?"

"I have to. Red says he can have my truck finished on Saturday, and my brothers wired money to pay him off." Connor reached over and took one of Keeley's hands in his. "So I need to leave then. I'm sorry."

She leaned against the back of the park bench and felt as if the breath had been stolen from her lungs.

"We probably won't ever see you here in town again, then."

"Not for a while, anyway. I have to go—for my son's sake." Connor swallowed hard. "I don't want him sitting in an apartment alone day after day while Marsha and her boyfriend are at work or spending their time at the casinos. I just can't let that happen. Not anymore."

Keeley's heart faltered as his words sank in. She'd known this day would come…yet the realization now settled over her like a dark and dismal fog.

"Of course. You need to do what's right for your son above all things. He's a very fortunate little guy," she said lightly, trying for a smile. "But I'll miss you. A lot."

"I wish..." His voice trailed off as he studied her for a long moment, his eyes filled with regret and longing. "I wish all things were possible. Honestly, I do."

He hesitated, then kissed her lightly on the cheek. Then he pulled her into his arms for a longer, deeper kiss that told her just how much he cared.

And then he walked away.

Chapter Twenty-One

Finding people to provide references in a hurry, plus completing a five-page questionnaire and a one-page written summary, had been the easy part.

By late Thursday afternoon Keeley had also been through two home visits and three interviews by various people with Child Protection Services.

The news that she'd passed with flying colors had filled her with momentary relief. But now, standing at the door of Bess's house, she felt a surge of doubt. Did she even want to be a part of breaking the older woman's heart?

The county would handle all of the details of this short-term foster arrangement. There was no need for her to be here, and maybe she was even breaking some protocol, but she needed to know, firsthand, that it would be all right.

Connor insisted on coming with her to make sure she was safe, though during daylight hours the run-down neighborhood looked more depressing than dangerous.

With Connor at her side, Keeley knocked on Bess's door. She waited a few minutes then knocked again.

Finally she heard the sound of shuffling feet and then a wrinkled face appeared in the window set in the door. A chain jingled and the door opened wide.

"Come in, come in," Bess said, stepping aside. "Both of you."

"Is, um, Rafe here?"

Bess shook her head. "He comes and he goes. No idea where he is or when he'll be back, but I kinda like it when he's gone."

"It's good to see you again," Keeley murmured.

"Don't mind the clutter. Things are a little out of order, but I've been cleaning today." Bess leaned forward with a conspiratorial twinkle in her eye. "That county home-aide gal comes today to do some cleaning, but I always want to pick up before she gets here."

Hiding a smile, Keeley took a chair next to a doily-topped end table while Connor stood sentry just inside the door, apparently watching out for Rafe. "I hear you were ill. How are you feeling?"

Bess waved off her concern. "It's just the diabetes. Must've got my insulin wrong—or maybe I didn't eat right."

"Goodness. That could be dangerous, Bess."

"So they say. Now there's *another* county gal coming once a week. She fixes my pillboxes and draws up my insulin for each day. A lot of foolishness, but that's what makes those folks happy."

"If she keeps you out of the ER, then that's wonderful, right?"

"It'll do, for now." Bess looked around the dimly lit living room and sighed. "They tell me I'd be better off in a senior apartment, and I suppose they're right. A lady from the county took me for a tour yesterday, and some of those places are mighty nice. I even have some old friends at the one over by Christmas Lake."

"That sounds lovely."

"But if I go to an old folks' home, I can't take Bobby.

He's been with me a long time. Me and Rafe are the only family he has left. With his special needs, how could anyone else love him like I do?" She lifted a trembling hand to her mouth. "But it is what it is, as they say. Bobby's gone all day at school, and they say I'm not safe here alone. And he needs someone who can take better care of him."

"He loves you, you know, and he always will. He's a very sweet boy," Keeley murmured.

"His social worker came by this morning. She said you agreed to take him for a while, until they can find a permanent foster home." Bess looked up at Keeley, her eyes shimmering with tears. "Is that true? Are you willing to do that for him?"

"Absolutely. And I promise that I'll bring him to see you every week. I could even do that when he's in his new home, if need be."

"Then it will be all right. Everything will be all right." Bess knotted her hands in her lap. "I used to hope he could be adopted after I couldn't take care of him any longer. I thought I could die happy if I just knew he had a real family and wouldn't be alone after he turned eighteen. But now he's sixteen and there's no hope of that, so this is surely the next best thing. Thank you, thank you—from the bottom of my heart."

And with that, Keeley's last shred of doubt melted away.

On Friday morning at ten o'clock Keeley sank onto the bench in front of her store and watched the county building inspector examine every last detail of the exterior, then go inside, a clipboard in hand.

With all of the smaller projects Connor had taken care of, plus all that the contractor and his team had tackled, everything should be in good order.

She hoped.

With such an old building, who could be sure? The electrical system was entirely new, the plumbing completely replaced, the roof was good and the floors were solid. Even the accessibility accommodations had been completed.

She'd taken care of everything listed in the initial report and more. *Please, God, let everything be all right.*

What would she do about the loan coming due and the refinancing if the building didn't pass inspection? The thought made her stomach tie itself into a knot.

Unable to sit still any longer, she jogged over to her dad's house and checked on him and the beef stew she'd started in his Crock-Pot this morning. Then she jogged back to the store and resumed her position on the bench.

The inspector, a tall, lean man with salt-and-pepper hair, finally stepped out of the building at two.

She jumped to her feet. "Is everything all right? Did it pass?"

"I need to write up my report first, then give copies to you and the bank," he said, his voice firm. A corner of his mouth twitched. "But I can tell you that it's good news."

"Really? It really passed?" Joy rushed through her. "When will those reports be done?"

"Well…this is my last appointment of the week." He shrugged. "Maybe later today, if I put you at the top of my stack."

Almost dizzy with excitement and relief, she flew through the rest of the afternoon, impatient to leave for the day and do…what?

She sobered.

Dad had supper waiting in his Crock-Pot so she and Connor could have a last dinner alone.

It would be a night to celebrate the end of renovations and a successful building inspection, though with Connor's departure for Texas tomorrow, the celebration would be bittersweet.

She didn't even want to think about the days and weeks… and months ahead without him.

Once he fell back into his old life at the ranch and renewed relationships with his dad and brothers, she guessed he would soon forget about the time he'd spent in a little town in Wisconsin.

He'd forget about her.

She closed the store early, grabbed the deposit bag with the day's earnings and strolled to the bank. After taking care of the deposit, she stopped at a secretary's desk at the end of the hall, where a young blonde was studying her computer screen.

"I have an appointment with Mr. Grover in two weeks, but I wonder if I can move it up," she said with a smile. "Any chance of that?"

"Have a seat and let me check," the blonde chirped. "I think I left his calendar by the copier."

She disappeared down the hallway and Keeley sank into the deep, plushy barrel chair to wait.

A man spoke in a hushed tone from behind the half-closed door of an office next to the receptionist's desk. "Did you see that inspection report?"

Keeley stiffened. It could be for any number of other projects, but still…

"Yeah, never thought that old building would pass, but there it is. That gal has done an amazing job with the place."

She stilled, filled with sudden hope. Could it be? Were her worries over?

The voice continued. "I'm still not sure about her low credit rating…"

"I don't know. If I remember right, she was hit by identity theft last winter and also had a credit card stolen. Tough luck."

"That building of hers housed a prosperous business for many years. Kinda nice to have that sense of heritage in town, don't you think? With so many businesses being taken over by newcomers?"

"Is her dad cosigning?"

The other man snickered. "I hope not. I don't know of a more difficult person to deal with. I never want to— Shut the door, will you?"

Then she heard the door close and their voices were too muffled to hear.

Keeley closed her eyes, imagining the rest of that conversation. Offering up a silent prayer.

Dad's finances had been a mess when she'd first come back to town. He'd fallen deeper and deeper into debt as his dementia slowly advanced, and this was where he did his banking. Could they somehow hold that against her in her loan application?

Surely not, since she was thirty-one and independent... though if they considered her a bad risk, would she ever know the true reasons for a denial?

A few minutes later the door by the receptionist's desk opened. Keeley stood, turned, and there stood Sam Grover with a junior associate she didn't recognize. "Hello, gentlemen."

The younger man's eyes flared open wide as he glanced between her and Grover, and then he mumbled an excuse and hurried down the hall.

"I came in to see about moving up my refinancing appointment with you, and couldn't help but overhear your conversation," she said. "I'm so glad to hear that my inspection went well. I've been working really hard to make sure everything measured up."

"Um, yes, yes, it did." Grover cleared his throat, a ruddy blush crawling upward above his collar. "The secretary must be around here somewhere—she can help you with your appointment."

"I also couldn't help but hear my dad come up in your conversation."

Clearly embarrassed by his careless verbal exchange within hearing, the man averted his gaze.

"You do understand that the building is in my name alone, right? I do know my father may be difficult to deal with at times, and that he recently ran into financial problems due to his dementia. But he owns no part of my building and will not ever be a part of the financial arrangements for my business in any way. So any past dealings with him will not impact my loan, right?"

The man's lips thinned. "No, of course not."

She gave him a warm smile. "That's wonderful news. Because otherwise, I'll be wanting an appointment with the bank president to discuss this further."

At five o'clock Keeley changed into her favorite ivory cashmere sweater and black linen slacks, freshened her makeup and fluffed her hair.

Anticipation for the evening ahead hummed through her veins as she donned a pair of pearl earrings and studied herself in the bathroom mirror.

Not too dressy, not too casual, so she'd fit right in with whatever Connor wore and wherever he wanted to go for a Friday-night dinner that would be both a celebration and a farewell. This would be the last time she might see him in…

Maybe forever.

At that sobering thought she felt her heart clench as she spritzed her favorite Burberry perfume on her wrists and then grabbed her purse and headed for the front of the store.

He was standing just inside the entryway, his Resistol hat in his hand and his mouth set in a grim line.

A faint smile touched his lips but didn't reach his eyes. "You look beautiful, Keeley. You flat-out take my breath away."

She took in his softly worn jeans and black oxford shirt with the cuffs folded back above his wrists and managed an answering grin despite her escalating trepidation. Something was wrong.

He strode up to her, his intent gaze locked on hers, and tossed his hat on the front counter before taking her into his arms with a low groan. "I've looked forward to this evening for days. *Days.*"

She leaned back to search his face. "Me, too. So what's wrong?"

He released her, stepped back. "It's my dad. I got a call from my brothers an hour ago. He's been taken to a hospital by ambulance and the docs think it's a heart attack."

"I'm so sorry," she breathed, taking in the ravaged look in his eyes. "Is he going to be all right?"

"They don't know yet." He dragged a palm down his face. "Red finished the truck this afternoon and I was already packed for tomorrow, but I can't wait until then. It's a fifteen-hour drive, and if I leave now I can get there by midmorning tomorrow."

She pressed her fingertips to her mouth. "You'll drive all night? Is that even safe?"

He shrugged. "I've got a twelve-pack of Coke on the front seat of my truck. With the radio blasting and the windows open, I should be fine."

He glanced toward the door and she knew he was on the

verge of bolting for his truck. "I—I know you must really want to see him, after all your time away."

"There's too much unfinished business between us—too much that's been left unsaid. If I can just get home in time..." His voice trailed off as he closed his eyes briefly.

She reached up and laid a hand gently against his cheek. "I will be praying you have safe travels. And that your dad will be well, too."

There was so much more she wanted to say to him. About how much she cared. How much she wanted him to come back to her. How much...she'd come to love him.

But he was radiating tension and worry, and this wasn't the time or place. "Godspeed, Connor. Be safe."

He pulled his truck keys from his front jeans' pocket, started for the door, then spun around and wrapped his arms around her. "I'll miss you," he whispered against her hair. "So doggone much."

And then he was gone.

Shell-shocked, Keeley stumbled up the stairs to her apartment and flopped on her bed to stare at the ceiling.

She'd known Connor was just passing through from the very beginning. She'd known that it would be pointless to let herself care.

And yet every passing day had shown her new and wonderful things about him. His kindness and patience toward her dad, and to Bobby. His honor, his work ethic and simple honesty. His gentleness.

And then there was the way her traitorous heart had chugged into overdrive whenever he'd walked into a room.

She'd sensed that he'd felt the same toward her, yet now he was driving away after a kiss and barely a goodbye.

She understood his reasons. After years of estrangement from his family, he couldn't risk arriving too late to see his father still alive.

But had he meant what he said—was he ever really coming back?

Numb, she tried to read, but stared at the pages blindly. She started to clean and then tossed the dust cloth aside.

She was on her third consolation bar of milk chocolate with hazelnuts and raisins when she heard the sound of crying and someone beating on the door downstairs. She ran down the steps and peered through the peephole, then flung the door wide open.

Bobby flew in and wrapped his arms around her.

"I—I th-think he killed her," he wailed, tears streaming down his face. "He came home and he was drunk and she told him to l-leave. And he hit her w-with the lamp. I *saw*."

Her heart thudding, Keeley stepped out of his embrace and grasped both of his shoulders. Shaking like an aspen leaf, he buckled to the floor. "Bobby. Did you call 9-1-1?"

He cried even harder. "There was blood everywhere and I r-ran. He was yelling at me to come b-back. B-but he was gonna hit me, t-too."

She grabbed the cell phone from her pocket and called 9-1-1.

After locking the dead bolts on the front and back doors and pulling down the shades, she sank to the floor next to him, set her phone aside and pulled him into her arms.

"The EMTs and the sheriff are on their way, honey. They'll take care of your auntie and they'll stop Rafe from ever doing anything bad again. I promise."

He cried even harder, his sobs coming in great waves, and she wondered about the demons this might have unearthed from the earlier tragedy in his life when his parents died. This was so terribly, horribly, unfair.

"It'll be okay, honey. I told them you're safe with me, and that you can stay the night here. I have your new room ready, so you can pretend you're camping at my house. Okay?"

She rubbed his back gently until his racking sobs slowed. "Let's go upstairs and have some hot chocolate, okay? I even have marshmallows. We can say some prayers for your aunt, and then you can tell me if you'd like to watch a movie or play some board games."

After two rounds of Chutes and Ladders and a card game of Old Maid, Bobby had settled down, clearly exhausted. She showed him the bathroom then got him settled into bed.

But still there'd been no word from anyone about Bess. What was going on? Or would no one think to call her? She wasn't family, so maybe not.

She'd just stepped out into the hallway to grab another cup of cocoa for herself when she heard a sound downstairs.

A crash.

The squeaky hinges on the front door and the soft jangle of the bells.

Then heavy footsteps started crossing the floor.

Chapter Twenty-Two

Connor gripped the steering wheel, his gaze pinned on the road ahead.

No one had called him a second time to let him know about his father's tests in the ER or his prognosis—or if he was still alive. But there was no question that Connor had to get home.

Connor had been praying ever since that first call. *Please, Lord, let me get there in time... He and I have so much to say...so much unfinished business. I need to get there.*

He could make the trip straight through in fifteen hours, according to the map function in his phone. But if he got a call about Dad being critical, he'd head for the Minneapolis-St. Paul airport, park the truck and take the first plane possible.

Connor tried calling Chris's cell phone and then Dan's. No answer. He tried again and again…

Then, finally, Dan picked up, his voice hushed. "Hey, man. You got the message?"

Connor swiftly pulled to a stop on the shoulder and turned on his emergency blinkers. "What's going on? How is Dad?"

Dan blew out a deep breath. "We've been in the ER for several hours now. Dad had severe heart pain, so we called the ambulance. They've been doing a lot of tests. Honestly, it has been a terrible afternoon. Dad was sort of out of it for a while and not making sense, and he kept calling for you. Kept saying he was sorry, and he didn't plan to die without making amends."

Connor's own heart felt as if it was lodged in his throat. "Any results? What do the doctors say?"

"Angina. Not a heart attack. They've got him resting comfortably right now. They plan to do more tests and keep him overnight, but he'll probably go home tomorrow."

Connor sagged against the seatback of his truck. "I can't tell you how relieved I am."

"Yeah. Me, too." Dan chuckled softly. "His doc told him that he was good for another thirty years, because he was too mean to die. Dad took it as a compliment. Hey—they're just now wheeling him back in from an MRI and we're not supposed to use cell phones in here. I'll call back in an hour or so. And, hey, bro—we're all real glad you're coming home. But don't push it and have a wreck. It's no longer an emergency to get here. Okay?"

The phone connection went dead.

Connor rubbed a hand over his face, exhaustion washing through him. *Thank You. Thank You, Lord.*

Darkness had fallen. He could continue driving throughout the night as he'd planned. The sooner he got to Texas, the better.

He had no other viable choice for establishing himself as quickly.

Otherwise his precarious hold on a future with Joshua could go up in smoke. On the twenty-thousand-acre Rafferty ranch in Texas, he would again be a part of a successful family business; his history would be a nonissue. By slipping back into the fabric of the family ranch it would be easy to prove to the court that he had a solid means of providing for his son again.

But even as he repeated that litany of reasons over and over to himself, an image of Keeley flashed into his thoughts as he continued down the highway. The temptation to turn around grew stronger, even though he knew that he had no future there.

He'd heard the whispers back in Aspen Creek. Knew that his past would always weigh heavily if he applied for jobs. Whether he'd been exonerated or not, there would always be the suspicions. The wary looks.

He kept driving south, but now the gnawing pain in his gut and an insistent voice in his head said otherwise. How could he leave Keeley behind? Was this really the right thing to do?

She'd welcomed him into her life. Given him a job.

Thanks to her, he'd experienced the normalcy that he'd lacked for years, giving him a chance for a fresh start. She'd trusted him, made him feel whole.

Still, there was no way he could support himself and his son in that little tourist town. And he knew she couldn't join him in Texas. Her connections in Wisconsin went as deep as the roots of the massive old oak by her store.

He drove on and on and on, his thoughts warring and his resolve weakening.

Until he finally drove onto a side road, parked and gave himself up to a heartfelt prayer.

I know I quit on You for a long time...and I'm sorry for that. But now I need Your help, because I have no idea which way I should go and what I should do. I can't risk losing my son, and I just can't lose Keeley. Please, Lord... tell me what to do.

* * *

Her heart in her throat, Keeley picked up the landline phone in the kitchen. No dial tone. She hung up and tried again. Tapped the zero for Operator and jiggled the phone line connection.

Dead.

Where was her cell phone? With growing horror she remembered calling 9-1-1…then setting it on the floor when she'd comforted Bobby. It was downstairs. There was no way to call for help.

And now they were trapped.

She could hear the footsteps grow louder as an intruder roamed through the main floor. Knocking things over. Throwing merchandise against the walls. Was he looking for something valuable to take? Could this be the guy who had been stealing from the stores in town?

He started jiggling doorknobs. Jerking doors open and slamming them shut. Searching. Then he uttered a string of curses and she knew this wasn't just some petty thief.

This was Rafe. He was drunk.

And he blamed her for contacting the sheriff's office when he'd hurt Bess. He also might be coming after Bobby.

When he found the right door, he could splinter it with one slam of his burly shoulder and come barging up the stairs.

Was he crazy enough to harm Bobby and her?

There would be no one to save them. No one who would even notice something was wrong until someone thought it curious that the store didn't open tomorrow.

She swallowed hard. Then went to Bobby's bedroom door and rapped lightly before walking in to shake his shoulder.

He sat up with a start, his eyes wide with fear. Then he focused on her face and relaxed. "I forgot where I was."

"You're here with me, Bobby," she said in a whisper. "But you need to do me a big favor and come with me right now. Don't say a single word, okay? Just come with me right now."

He grabbed her arm. "Why? What's wrong?"

She forced herself to stay calm. "I think Rafe is downstairs and I want to get you out of here. Understand? We're going to the balcony off the kitchen. The fire escape needs another part, so we can't use it yet. But there's a rope ladder we can drop that nearly touches the ground, and when you get down I want you to run fast as you can to the sheriff's office. Do you know where that is?"

He gave a single nod and swallowed hard, his face pale. "By the store with the canoes and bikes."

"That's right. Someone is there 24/7. Tell them Rafe is here and there's trouble."

The door at the bottom of the stairs crashed open and footsteps started up. Slowly, as if Rafe were too inebriated to manage the climb.

Please, God, stop him. Slow him down—anything.

She grabbed Bobby's hand and dragged him through the living room and kitchen, quietly opened the French door to the balcony and tossed the rope ladder over the side.

"Now go. Hurry!"

"I can't leave without you," he cried, staring nervously at the ground far below. "You go first."

"I won't go until you do, in case I have to hold Rafe back. Now hurry. *Please.*"

Bobby finally registered the need for urgency and awkwardly climbed over the balcony railing. He gripped the top of the rope ladder and floundered until his feet found the first rung.

He froze, his face a mask of terror.

"Go, Bobby!"

He slowly descended, his eyes closed, each rung a painstaking effort. The rope ladder creaked and twisted under his weight.

"Good boy," she whispered.

She turned away for one last look toward the stairway door—

Rafe's twisted, malevolent face loomed over her, his breath laced with stale beer. "That boy ruined my life, and you let him get away," he snarled.

With an enraged bellow he swung his fist. The pain in her head exploded in a shower of blinding sparks. She reeled backward against the door frame and slid to the floor.

Through half-closed eyes she saw him smirk with satisfaction. Then he turned toward the stairway to the first floor. Her stomach lurched at the thought of dear old Bess. Was Bobby right about Bess or had the EMTs arrived in time? *Please, Lord, help Bess...and Bobby...*

She heard more sounds downstairs—footsteps running through the store. "Keeley! Are you all right? Where are you?"

Connor.

Rafe heard him, too, because he halted abruptly on his way to the stairs, then pivoted and looked wildly around the room. He lurched toward the French door to the balcony and disappeared into the darkness.

"Not safe—" she shouted.

But a second later she heard the sound of splintering wood. The screech of twisting, rusted iron giving way. A scream.

And then a heavy thud.

"Are you *sure* Bess will be all right?"

The ER nurse smiled at Keeley and patted her arm. "I'm

very sure. She has some bumps and bruises, and needed a few stitches. But she's a remarkably resilient woman. Her husband wasn't quite so lucky with that fire escape. He'll be in traction for months."

Keeley held back a smile. "I did try to warn him it wasn't safe."

"He won't be causing any trouble for a good long while." Deputy Dalton had arrived a few minutes ago, his face grim. "When he gets out of the hospital he'll be in jail. We've got enough on him now to put him away for quite a while, and Lorraine discovered outstanding warrants on him in Illinois." He turned to Keeley. "Are you sure you're all right?"

Keeley nestled deeper into Connor's embrace on the waiting-room sofa. "A bit of a headache, maybe. If Connor hadn't arrived when he did, things could have been so much worse."

"And Bobby was quite a hero himself," Connor added, giving the boy a nod of approval.

Bobby beamed. "I went down the rope ladder and found the deputy. I even got to ride in his car, with the siren and everything."

Dalton touched the brim of his cap. "Well, folks, I've got to go."

"Thanks, for everything." After he left, Keeley shifted in Connor's embrace so she could look up at him. "I was so shocked when I heard your voice, I could barely believe it—but I still don't understand why you came back so soon."

Bobby blushed, the tips of his ears turning bright red. "Because he likes you. He *really* likes you."

She grinned at him. "I really hope you're right."

"I still need to go to Texas for a while. But I'll do my best to find a job here—there has to be *something* I can do. And I just couldn't leave without telling you the truth."

Connor stood and gently pulled her to her feet. He took a slow, steadying breath, his eyes locked on hers. "I love you, Keeley. I think I've loved you from that very first day when I walked into your store."

Joy spread through her like a burst of fireworks, so dazzling and overwhelming that it took her a moment to speak. "I've never believed in love at first sight. I haven't even believed in love, really…not for me. But now I know—no one else was perfect because none of them was you."

She framed his face within her hands and kissed him, sighing softly when he wrapped his arms around her and returned her kiss in full measure.

When they finally ended the embrace, the jaded heart that had never allowed itself to love was nearly bursting. "I love you, too, Connor. Forever and always."

Epilogue

Six months later

Connor pulled off his gloves, jammed them into his back pocket and hooked his boot on the lower rail of the white fence. "So what do you think?"

Out in the corral, Bobby and Joshua were mounted on elderly, well-broken mares, and from the boys' delighted laughter and banter, they were enjoying every minute.

Connor hadn't been back in town long before he'd asked Keeley about providing formal foster care for Bobby… and now they were working on the possibility of adoption.

"I think our guys are having a wonderful time. And I still have to pinch myself to remember that this is all real. My dad really came through, didn't he?"

"He sure did."

Paul had asked him one day about his job skills and Connor had rattled off his past life on the ranch, followed by the rodeo circuit. He'd forgotten about that conversation.

But for all that Paul struggled with dementia, he had remembered. He'd begun asking questions.

And through a friend of a friend who knew someone else, he'd learned of a wealthy, nationally known quarter-horse breeder not far from Aspen Creek, who had been advertising in *The Quarter Horse Journal* for months, trying to find a good trainer and ranch manager.

"Are you ever sorry you didn't go back to Texas?"

Connor smiled. "Never. Staying here meant being with you, and that means far more to me. I can always go south for another visit, and they're planning to come up. But this is where I belong. With all of you."

He reached in his back pocket and pulled out a small box. His heart pounded in his throat and his hand shook when he offered it to her.

"I've been waiting a long time to do this. I needed to feel worthy of you, and now I hope I am. Keeley, will you marry me?"

Suddenly breathless, she stared at his hand in shock. *"Really?"*

The boys trotted the mares across the arena and pulled to a stop next to them. "Did you do it, Dad?" Josh stood in his stirrups for a better view. "Did she say yes?"

Keeley looked up at Connor, her eyes glistening with tears. Then she opened the box and cried out with delight. "It's gorgeous. Absolutely gorgeous! I can't believe it— Where— How—"

"The shoplifters were finally caught—a group of high-school girls in town. They had held on to everything they'd stolen. Then one had the bright idea to take some loot to a pawnshop. They tried to sell the garnet ring they stole from you." He toed at a clump of grass. "I'll replace those garnets with diamonds as soon as I can, but I was sorta figuring we'd need to buy a house."

She shook her head. "This is what I want. The ring is beautiful and it means so much to me that I never want to let it go."

She slid it on her finger. Then walked into his arms

and gave him a long kiss. "My answer is yes—always and forever, yes."

And in that moment he knew that he could never regret anything in his life that had brought him to this town and this woman.

Because he was well and truly home at last.

* * * * *

If you loved this story,
pick up the other ASPEN CREEK CROSSROADS
books from beloved author Roxanne Rustand:

WINTER REUNION
SECOND CHANCE DAD

Available now from Love Inspired!

Find more great reads at www.LoveInspired.com

COMING NEXT MONTH FROM
Love Inspired®

Available July 19, 2016

A BEAU FOR KATIE
The Amish Matchmaker • by Emma Miller

An accident leaves Freeman Kemp with a broken leg—and no choice but to find a housekeeper. He never imagines that hiring Katie Byler will turn his household—and his heart—upside down.

THE TEXAN'S SECOND CHANCE
Blue Thorn Ranch • by Allie Pleiter

Determined to overcome his black-sheep reputation, Witt Buckton takes command of Blue Thorn Ranch's new food-truck business. Hiring the talented Jana Powers as head chef will bring him one step closer to success—and to love.

HER UNEXPECTED FAMILY
Grace Haven • by Ruth Logan Herne

Single dad Grant McCarthy is all about family—even taking on planning his sister's wedding while she's deployed overseas. As he falls for wedding planner Emily Gallagher, can he also make room in his life for a wife?

THE BACHELOR'S SWEETHEART
The Donnelly Brothers • by Jean C. Gordon

They've always been just friends, but when Josh Donnelly and Tessa Hamilton team up to renovate her movie theater, their feelings deepen. Will their blossoming romance survive after Tessa reveals a dark secret she's kept hidden?

SMALL-TOWN GIRL
Goose Harbor • by Jessica Keller

Starting over in Goose Harbor, Kendall Mayes opens her dream business, which brings her into contact with handsome loner Brice Daniels. But everything could fall apart if he discovers her secret business partner is the man he hates most.

LAKESIDE ROMANCE
by Lisa Jordan

Sarah Sullivan's new life plan involves making a success of her church's summer community outreach program—and excludes love. Until she asks Alec Seaver to help teach her charges how to cook—and begins to reconsider a future that includes her handsome neighbor.

LOOK FOR THESE AND OTHER LOVE INSPIRED BOOKS WHEREVER BOOKS ARE SOLD, INCLUDING MOST BOOKSTORES, SUPERMARKETS, DISCOUNT STORES AND DRUGSTORES.

LICNM0716

REQUEST YOUR FREE BOOKS!

2 FREE INSPIRATIONAL NOVELS PLUS 2 FREE MYSTERY GIFTS

Love Inspired®

YES! Please send me 2 FREE Love Inspired® novels and my 2 FREE mystery gifts (gifts are worth about $10). After receiving them, if I don't wish to receive any more books, I can return the shipping statement marked "cancel." If I don't cancel, I will receive 6 brand-new novels every month and be billed just $4.99 per book in the U.S. or $5.49 per book in Canada. That's a saving of at least 17% off the cover price. It's quite a bargain! Shipping and handling is just 50¢ per book in the U.S. and 75¢ per book in Canada.* I understand that accepting the 2 free books and gifts places me under no obligation to buy anything. I can always return a shipment and cancel at any time. Even if I never buy another book, the two free books and gifts are mine to keep forever.

105/305 IDN GH5P

Name (PLEASE PRINT)

Address Apt. #

City State/Prov. Zip/Postal Code

Signature (if under 18, a parent or guardian must sign)

Mail to the **Reader Service:**

IN U.S.A.: P.O. Box 1867, Buffalo, NY 14240-1867

IN CANADA: P.O. Box 609, Fort Erie, Ontario L2A 5X3

Are you a subscriber to Love Inspired® books and want to receive the larger-print edition? Call 1-800-873-8635 or visit www.ReaderService.com.

* Terms and prices subject to change without notice. Prices do not include applicable taxes. Sales tax applicable in N.Y. Canadian residents will be charged applicable taxes. Offer not valid in Quebec. This offer is limited to one order per household. Not valid for current subscribers to Love Inspired books. All orders subject to credit approval. Credit or debit balances in a customer's account(s) may be offset by any other outstanding balance owed by or to the customer. Please allow 4 to 6 weeks for delivery. Offer available while quantities last.

Your Privacy—The Reader Service is committed to protecting your privacy. Our Privacy Policy is available online at www.ReaderService.com or upon request from the Reader Service.

We make a portion of our mailing list available to reputable third parties that offer products we believe may interest you. If you prefer that we not exchange your name with third parties, or if you wish to clarify or modify your communication preferences, please visit us at www.ReaderService.com/consumerschoice or write to us at Reader Service Preference Service, P.O. Box 9062, Buffalo, NY 14240-9062. Include your complete name and address.

LI15

SPECIAL EXCERPT FROM

Love Inspired®

When a handsome Amish mill owner breaks his leg, a feisty young Amish woman agrees to be his housekeeper. But will two weeks together lead to romance or heartbreak?

Read on for a sneak preview of
A BEAU FOR KATIE,
the third book in Emma Miller's miniseries
***THE AMISH MATCHMAKER*.**

"Here's Katie," Sara the matchmaker announced. "She'll lend a hand with the housework until you're back on your feet." She motioned Katie to approach the bed. "I think you two already know each other."

"*Ya,*" Freeman admitted gruffly. "We do."

Katie removed her black bonnet. Freeman Kemp wasn't hard on the eyes. Even lying flat in a bed, one leg in a cast, he was still a striking figure of a man. The pain lines at the corners of his mouth couldn't hide his masculine jaw. His wavy brown hair badly needed a haircut, and he had at least a week's growth of dark beard, but the cotton undershirt revealed broad, muscular shoulders and arms.

Freeman's compelling gaze met hers. His eyes were brown, almost amber, with darker swirls of color. Unnerved, she uttered in a hushed tone, "Good morning, Freeman."

Then Katie turned away to inspect the kitchen that would be her domain for the next two weeks. She'd never been inside the house before, but from the outside, she'd thought it was beautiful. Now, standing in the spacious kitchen, she liked it even more. The only thing that looked out of place was the bed containing the frowning Freeman.

"You must be in a lot of pain," Sara remarked, gently patting Freeman's cast.

"*Ne*. Nothing to speak of."

Katie nodded. "Well, rest and proper food for an invalid will do you the most good."

Freeman glanced away. "I'm *not* an invalid."

Katie sighed. If your leg encased in a cast didn't make you an invalid, she didn't know what did. But Freeman, as she recalled, had a stubborn nature.

For an eligible bachelor who owned a house, a mill and two hundred acres of prime land to remain single into his midthirties was almost unheard of among the Amish. Add to that, Freeman's rugged good looks. It made him the catch of the county. They could have him. She was not a giggling teenager who could be swept off her feet by a pretty face. Working in his house for two whole weeks wasn't going to be easy, but he didn't intimidate her. She'd told Sara she'd take the job and she was a woman of her word.

Don't miss
A BEAU FOR KATIE by Emma Miller,
available August 2016 wherever
Love Inspired® books and ebooks are sold.

www.LoveInspired.com

Copyright © 2016 by Emma Miller

LIEXP0716

SPECIAL EXCERPT FROM

Love Inspired® HISTORICAL

With her uncle trying to claim her ranch, widow Lula May Barlow has no time to worry about romance. But can she resist Edmund McKay—the handsome cowboy next door—when he helps her fight for her land…and when her children start playing matchmaker?

Read on for a sneak preview of A FAMILY FOR THE RANCHER, the heartwarming continuation of the series ***LONE STAR COWBOY LEAGUE: THE FOUNDING YEARS***

"Just wanted to return your book."

Book?

Lula May saw her children slinking out of the barn, guilty looks on their faces. So that's why they'd made such nuisances of themselves out at the pasture. They'd wanted her to send them off to play so they could take the book to Edmund. And she knew exactly why. Those little rascals were full-out matchmaking! Casting a look at Edmund, she faced the inevitable, which wasn't really all that bad. "Will you come in for coffee?"

He tilted his hat back to reveal his broad forehead, where dark blond curls clustered and made him look younger than his thirty-three years. "Coffee would be good."

Lula May led him in through the back door. To her horror, Uncle sat at the kitchen table hungrily eyeing the cake she'd made for Edmund…and almost forgotten about. Now she'd have no excuse for not introducing them before she figured out how to get rid of Floyd.

"Edmund, this is Floyd Jones." She forced herself to add, "My uncle. Floyd, this is my neighbor, Edmund McKay."

As the children had noted last week when Edmund first

LIHEXP0716

stepped into her kitchen, he took up a good portion of the room. Even Uncle seemed a bit unsettled by his presence. While the men chatted about the weather, however, Lula May could see the old wiliness and false charm creeping into Uncle's words and facial expressions. She recognized the old man's attempt to figure Edmund out so he could control him.

Pauline and Daniel worked at the sink, urgent whispers going back and forth. Why had they become so bold in their matchmaking? Was it possible they sensed the danger of Uncle's presence and wanted to lure Edmund over here to protect her? She wouldn't have any of that. She'd find a solution without any help from anybody, especially not her neighbor. Her only regret was that she hadn't been able to protect the children from realizing Uncle wasn't a good man. If she could have found a way to be nicer to him… No, that wasn't possible. Not when he'd come here for the distinct purpose of seizing everything she owned.

The men enjoyed their coffee and cake, after which Edmund suggested they take a walk around the property to build up an appetite for supper.

"We'd like to go for a walk with you, Mr. McKay," Pauline said. "May we, Mama?"

Lula May hesitated. Let them continue their matchmaking or make them spend time with Uncle? Neither option pleased her. When had she lost control of her household? About a week before Uncle arrived, that was when, the day when Edmund had walked into her kitchen and invited himself into her…or rather, her eldest son's life.

"You may go, but don't pester Mr. McKay." She gave the children a narrow-eyed look of warning.

Their innocent blinks did nothing to reassure her.

Don't miss

A FAMILY FOR THE RANCHER

by Louise M. Gouge, available August 2016 wherever Love Inspired® Historical books and ebooks are sold.

www.LoveInspired.com

Copyright © 2016 by Harlequin Books, S.A.

LIHEXP0716

Inspirational Romance to Warm your Heart & Soul

Whether you love heart-pounding suspense, historically rich stories or contemporary heartfelt romances, Love Inspired® Books has it all!

Connect with us to find your next great read from the ***Love Inspired, Love Inspired Suspense*** and ***Love Inspired Historical*** series.

 www.Facebook.com/LoveInspiredBooks

www.Twitter.com/LoveInspiredBks

www.LoveInspired.com

LIHALOIBCR

The Cowboy's Second Chance

With the town's busiest sales weekend on the horizon, store owner Keeley North is desperate to find help. So when Connor Rafferty walks through her door, he's an unlikely answer to her prayers. The former rodeo star may be a fish out of water in her shop, but he can rise to any challenge. And right now he's set his sights on finding the son he hasn't seen in five years. Keeley can't risk her heart on a scarred cowboy who's searching for something more. But if she can convince him to look beyond the mistakes of his past, Connor may get a second chance to have it all.

ASPEN CREEK CROSSROADS:
Where faith, love and healing meet

$5.99 U.S./$6.75 CAN.

CATEGORY
INSPIRATIONAL

harlequin.com